CW00740700

John Creas

John Creasey, "The King of Crime," wrote 562 crime and mystery books in 41 years, making him the world's most prolific author.*

His books have sold more than 80 million copies worldwide in 28 languages and *The Creasey Dagger* is still the UK's top award for first time crime novelists. Past winners include Patricia Cornwell and Minette Walters. Creasey's most famous characters include *The Toff, The Baron, Inspector West* and *Gideon.*

John Creasey was also the founder of the All Party Alliance in England, a political movement advocating government by the best men from all the parties working together. He fought four by-elections in 1967/68.

He advocated not only shared political control of nations but industrial democracy in which workers, management (with marketing and research staff), private investors and the State (or Federal Union) shared ownership and control of all industry and commerce. He claimed that these systems would end political strife and reduce strikes, thus increasing national prosperity to the point where the State's profit could virtually do away with income tax.

* Barbara Cartland wrote more books than John Creasey—an average of eight books a year, totalling 623 in 77 years of writing. Creasey wrote 13 books per year in 41 years of writing, making him 171% more prolific.

For more about John Creasey, www.johncreasey.com

Other John Creasey titles from Tethered Camel Publishing:

Introducing The Toff
The Toff and the Curate
Accuse The Toff
The Toff and the Lady

LAST LAUGH FOR THE TOFF

John Creasey

CREASEY CRIME CLASSICS

Creasey Crime Classics
An imprint of Tethered Camel Publishing

Copyright © Siguy South 2004
First published in 1954 as *The Toff at the Fair*

The moral right of the author has been asserted

A CIP catalogue record for this book
is available from the British Library

ISBN 1-904612-13-X

Printed and bound by Selwood Printing Ltd.,
Burgess Hill, West Sussex

Jacket design by Mostra Ltd., Haymarket, London SW1

Tethered Camel Publishing
PO Box 12036, Bromsgrove, Worcs.
B60 1WT

Foreword

RICHARD CREASEY

The Toff—or the Honourable Richard Rollison—was "born" in the twopenny weekly *Thriller* in 1933 but it was not until 1938 that my father, John Creasey, first published books about him. At once the Toff took on characteristics all his own and became a kind of "*Saint* with his feet on the ground." My father consciously used the Toff to show how well the Mayfair man-about-town could get on with the rough diamonds of the East End.

What gives the Toff his ever-fresh, ever-appealing quality is that he likes people and continues to live a life of glamour and romance while constantly showing (by implication alone) that all men are brothers under the skin.

I am delighted that the Toff is available again to enchant a whole new audience. And proud that my parents named me Richard after such an amazing role-model.

Richard Creasey is Chairman of The Television Trust for the Environment *and, for the last 20 years, has been an executive producer for both BBC and ITV.*

It was John Creasey who introduced him to the world of travel and adventure. Richard and his brother were driven round the world for 465 days in the back of their parents' car when they were five and six years old. In 1992 Richard led 'The Overland Challenge' driving from London to New York via the Bering Strait.

CHAPTER ONE

Strong Man

' 'ERE YOU ARE, me lucky lads, three shies a tanner, take a milky coconut home to your Mum... Best South Sea Island coconuts, off wiv their 'eads and out pops a dusky maiden—ups-a-daisy! You, sir?'

A small young man with ginger hair flicked a sixpence into a palm of quite remarkable size. The corns and callouses on it were of little moment. The broad finger-tips, known to the erudite as spatulate, did not cause a second glance; the ingrained dirt of weeks—it could have been of months—meant nothing. The size of the hand was everything because it was at the end of a short arm and a narrow wrist and was attached to a small man.

'Roll up, roll up,' roared the owner of the hand, 'watch the 'eads roll! One...' He paused as the ginger-haired man, wooden ball in hand, drew his arm back... 'Two... three!... Blimey, leave a bit o' the canvas, mister.'

The ball smacked into the canvas backing and dropped to the grass. The second followed suit. The third struck a coconut but did not dislodge it.

'Bad luck, mister, like to try again?... Roll up, me lucky lads, don't forget the dusky damsel who's going to pop up—you, sir?' He beamed at a slim young man. 'Don't be afraid, show the lady that yer aim's as straight as yer 'eart!... Only a tanner for three loverly coconuts—'ere!'

The last was almost a screech of indignation.

The red-haired youth who had nearly won a coconut had calmly taken three more wooden balls out of the box on its stand; and was now taking fresh aim.

'Payment in advance, that's me motto!' roared the small man with the huge hand. 'Tanner for three shots, you ain't deaf.'

'You owe me a free turn,' said the ginger-haired man mildly. He had a most attractive smile and white, shiny teeth. He wore a browny-yellow coat and baggy green corduroys, brown shoes with huge crêpe-rubber soles.

'Stand aside,' he ordered and added, still smiling, 'My man.'

'Why, I'll—' began the coconut-shy huckster. In a careless moment he stretched out one of those fantastic hands to grasp the man with ginger hair. It was a mistake. It was a big mistake. His hand fell upon the shoulder of the colourful coat—and thus precipitated a pyrotechnic display that would have made Mr Brock of Crystal Palace turn green with envy. The ginger-haired man seemed to possess the secret of perpetual motion. He tossed the wooden balls back into the bin then struck the huckster gently in the stomach, as gently on the jaw, then spun him round by the shoulder and kicked him, still gently; then, as if he were warming up, he used both fists as battering rams and struck at chin, chest, and stomach. The speed of his attack was so bewildering, the ease of his conquest so astounding, that the dozen or so people in sight stood and stared.

With a final assault which he accomplished with insulting ease, the ginger-haired young man caught his victim's wrist, placed a leg behind the other's leg and twisted; the huckster turned a cartwheel, and crashed against the canvas which divided his stall from a rifle range.

'Next time, my lucky lad, don't use glue to stick the coconuts on with,' said the ginger-haired youth and beamed broadly. The sun shone on his teeth and hair, he was remarkable to look at; so bewilderingly small to be so tough. 'Because if you do—'

He broke off and a new light glowed in his eyes.

The balls used for hurling at the coconuts, which sat like bearded puppets on their spindle-shanked cups, reposed in the wooden box which was on a stand and close to him. He turned the box upside down. Fifty, a hundred, two hundred lightweight wooden balls fell out and rolled about the ground. The ginger-haired man picked up three and hurled them at the coconuts in quick succession.

Two nuts fell.

The huckster was picking himself up.

Several fairground men came running to find out what was wrong and an onlooker, a rough-looking, tough-looking bruiser type, seemed to catch the prevailing excitement and got in their way. Sentences, some cut in half, sounded above the general clamour.

'What the heck...?'

'Out of my way, mister!'

'Wot's up, Bert?'

'He tried...'

The ginger-haired young man had sauntered towards his coconuts. He picked them up and turned to survey the scene. In the two minutes or less since his back had been turned, it had been transformed. The spectators had been startled into movement. The rough and tough-looking man was using his arms like flails, two fairground workers were already on the scene. Others came running, shouting loudly.

The ginger-haired youth, with delightful nonchalance, tossed the coconuts among the crowd. A sane and sober judge would have said that he was drunk for only a drunk would indulge so earnestly in such pranks; for the coconuts fell on bare heads and hurt.

Then the fight started in earnest and, for a few golden minutes, it was difficult to see who was hitting whom.

The ginger-haired harbinger of trouble started playing football with the light wooden balls; two others joined in and more followed. Soon the balls were being kicked and dribbled all over the place. The fight was still waxing furiously and, above the nasal howl of the hurdy-gurdies and the Galloping Horses, the hissing roar of the switchback and the medley of voices imploring business, there came a new sound: a police whistle.

Two policeman came running.

Strong, happy men stopped fighting, gathered up the wooden balls hilariously and used them as snowballs, pelting police and spectators with strict impartiality. Then, suddenly and with malice, the ginger-haired youth hurled three balls in succession at a police-sergeant, turned tail and bolted.

How he could run.

The sign of defeat was a signal for others who were in a pugnacious or rumbustious mood to flee. The police, now half a dozen strong, found themselves with none but the innocent to deal with. The fairground men had come off badly, sharing bruised and discoloured eyes and torn clothes, but none was so bad as the coconut-shy huckster whose lips were cut and bleeding, whose right eye was swelling and whose right sleeve was almost torn out of his coat shoulder.

'...I never did a *thing*,' he asseverated dazedly and looked among the crowd as if hoping that no witness remained to testify that he had struck the first blow; or at least, raised the first hand in violence. 'Started taking shies without paying, he did. I only arst him...'

In spite of his injuries he gave a long, indignant and increasingly vituperative account of what had happened and called on unseen witnesses and heavenly bodies to corroborate his story. No one did, except vaguely. No one appeared to have seen his huge hand descend upon the red-haired youth's shoulder.

Except the girl.

She was young. She was pretty. She had a nice little figure, which an infidel or a cynic would call curvaceous, and the kind of beautiful legs and ankles which had given birth to the original wolf-whistle. She had very bright blue eyes and wavy dark hair, wore a bottle-green suit of smooth-textured cloth and lips which made the lovelorn think mostly of kisses.

'But Rolly,' she said to her companion in a tone which could only be called protesting, 'aren't you going to *say* something?'

The tall man by her side looked down on her. He would have attracted a great deal of attention even by himself because he was one of those favoured men whom Nature had adorned with outstanding good looks. His hair was dark and a narrow peaked cap, set at a jaunty angle, hid the few wiry flecks of grey which showed that youth was leaving him, if slowly. He had the kind of grey eyes that make people smile without quite knowing why. He had that kind of face, too—very handsome, tanned without being ostentatiously ruddy-hued, nice lips, a good chin. Added to all this he had a supple leanness of figure, long legs and narrow hips. His light-grey sports jacket with two slits near the hips told its own story; or seemed to. He was "county."

The girl's blue eyes burned indignantly at him.

'Aren't you going to *say* something?' she repeated.

'I am,' declared the man she had called Rolly and he looked more closely into her eyes. 'If I were ten years younger, I should carry you off here and now. You shouldn't be allowed. You remind me of lost youth and past conquests and how there was a time when a girl like you would have swooned in my arms.'

'Oh, you fool! You saw it, didn't you? That man over there started it and Micky...'

'And to make it worse, they call you Sal,' mourned the tall, lean man. 'Oh, Sal. No. Remember that you might have to say that in a magistrate's court and magistrates were ever sceptical of blue-eyed beauties whose hearts throb for red-haired—'

'Oh, you're impossible! And I really thought,' said Sal, only to pause, draw herself up to her full five feet four inches and repeat with searing derision, 'I really thought you were a detective !'

Nearby a large, heavy, brown-clad man with a cleft in his chin gave a gratified kind of smile.

'Are you going to tell the police it wasn't Micky's fault or aren't you?' demanded Sal and her voice became almost shrill again.

'The foolish are always with us,' said the man named Rolly and turned to wink at the man with a cleft, who looked startled for he had not known that he had been noticed. 'Sweet Sal, be wise. If the cops catch Micky and charge him, we can give evidence to get him off with a minimum sentence. If they don't catch him, it'll all blow over. Won't it, Tipple?'

The massive man with the cleft chin opened his mouth, rather as a man might open a trap-door.

'I don't think I quite caught what you said, Mr Rollison.'

'Oh, my Tipple,' reproved Rollison, 'your ears are as sharp as the ears of elephants.' He beamed. 'Come on, Sal.'

He placed a hand firmly on Sal's arm, just above the elbow, and led her away. She moved with the unconscious grace of youth and could make men catch their breath.

'Who was that?' she asked.

'That,' said Rollison, firmly, 'was and still is, to the distress of many bad men, Detective Inspector Wilfrid Tipple of the Criminal Investigation Department. Once the bad men have stopped laughing their heads off at a DI bearing such a name as Wilfrid Tipple, they find themselves in jail. He is very clever. I wish I knew why he was at Happy Hampstead.'

'This isn't Hampstead,' observed Sal and suddenly stopped and stared up at Rollison. Her head was a little on one side. Her eyes began to shoot fire again. Her lips seemed to demand attention. 'And they haven't, anyway!'

'I beg your pardon,' said Rollison.

'And I don't think much of your general knowledge.'

'Sal, I don't mind being blamed for what I do wrong, I don't even mind you deriding my hard-won reputation as a private eye, I gladly give way to Hawkshaw. But what's the matter with my general knowledge?'

'Elephants,' Sal said, witheringly.

'Oh,' said Rollison, faintly.

'And you ought to know,' declared Sal.

'Undoubtedly,' agreed Rollison. 'Indubitably. Let's go and get a drink or go for a walk or go home or something. I don't think Micky will stay long, do you?'

'Of course he won't. He'll be miles away by now. You don't know Micky!' Sal said that with pride.

'At moments I feel that I could rejoice about that. The bright boy with the coconuts probably felt the same.'

'Richard,' said Sal in a different, steely voice, 'there are certainly moments when I could dislike you acutely. Anyone would think that you were on that hulking brute's side and not on Micky's.'

She stalked ahead; or would have, if Rollison had not lengthened his stride so as to keep abreast of her. She did not look at him. They passed the huge marquee with its gay flags of all nations and its hideous pictures of lions and tigers and turned towards a path marked *Car Park* with Sal a yard in front.

She jumped and banged against Rollison.

'*Oooh!*' she gasped.

An elephant's trunk appeared from the side of the tent. It performed improbable circlings about the air and was then withdrawn. Subdued, Sal walked on until they were by the side of Rollison's car, a pearl grey Rolls-Bentley. He opened the door and Sal climbed in.

'Let us now get some things straight,' said Rollison, offering cigarettes which she refused disdainfully. 'We came to see your Micky because you're worried about him and because someone had told you that I was the great detective.'

'At least I know better now,' Sal said bitingly.

'And we found Micky at a distance,' continued Rollison, unperturbed. 'You think he's being blackmailed and that he pays his tribute to someone at the circus. But all we saw was a fracas and Micky showing off. A fool yet not a fool, your Mick.'

'Richard, if you—'

'You hired me, remember?' asked Rollison firmly. 'I am now a professional and you insisted on paying my fee. I still have your cheque in my pocket because you don't see why a cousin thrice removed—'

'Four *times* removed. I wish it were a million.'

'Far removed should be expected to slave without reward,' continued Rollison imperturbably. 'So my duty to my client compels me to report my findings. They are that Micky is a fool but not a fool. I should think he is somewhat swollen-headed but it might not have been conceit alone, it might have been sheer high spirits.'

Sal was glaring. 'Rolly, if you don't stop—'

Rollison was looking through the windscreen at two small boys climbing an oak tree in the wood near the car park.

He did not appear to notice Sal's interruption as he went on:

'First, he missed two coconuts, then scraped a third. The second time, when he helped himself to three shies, he was on the target each time. So why did he miss the others? Could it have been to pick a quarrel?'

'Oh, you're crazy!'

'And so turn the coconut man upside down and inside out?' asked Rollison mildly. 'And use the little wooden balls as footballs? I'd like to know. You ought to want to know, too.'

How she blazed at him.

'You're absolutely re*pul*sive. I simply wanted to help Mick and all you do is suggest that he—that he—'

'That he's a remarkable young man, first missing the coconuts and then hitting them, next committing assault and battery on the coconut boy, having been his own *agent provocateur*, and finally—do you want to hear finally?'

'No!'

'And finally, why did he walk off with one of the little wooden balls in his pocket?' asked Rollison earnestly.

CHAPTER TWO

Summons

SAL HARDY TOSSED her head, in the way of spoiled, pretty girls who are offended or affronted, and stared straight ahead of her. The road, leading to London, ran alongside the park near Kingston where the fair was gathering momentum for the evening orgies. It was a Saturday afternoon in June, the weather was chilly but the sky clear and promising warmth.

In silence, Rollison and Sal drove along, taking no notice of the huge circus tent, the marquees, the big crowds, the hurdy-gurdies, the giant wheel; or, for that matter, of anything. Most of the traffic was coming towards the fair and a stream of people, thickly sprinkled with children, passed the car. Many looked at it. Several turned to stare because Sal was really something to see and Rollison might have been a cavalier born out of his time. He sat in the princely car as a knight might have sat upon his snorting charger in the days of old and there was just such a look in his eyes.

They reached the Kingston by-pass. On the two-lane highway, Rollison could show what the Rolls-Bentley could do. It purred along at eighty. Sal still stared straight ahead of her, refusing to say a word, apparently determined not to thaw. Rollison glanced at her occasionally and each time his lips twitched. Near the Robin Hood Gate end of the by-pass she glanced also and, for a split second, their gaze met.

Sal's cheeks turned red.

'Sal,' murmured Rollison caressingly, by way of olive branch.

She continued to look straight ahead.

'I think you have been insufferable,' she said clearly. 'Your behaviour has been positively abominable. I am only sorry that I told you anything about it. I shall not tell you anything more and I have no wish to see you again.'

'Lucky Micky,' murmured Rollison.

Sal flared up. 'What do you mean?'

'The man who has your heart, sweet Sal, is one of the really lucky men,' Rollison said and swerved to avoid two cyclists who were moving along abreast, merrily unaware of the death at their heels.

Sal said, ' Don't try to smarm me over!'

'No, dear,' murmured Rollison.

He drove across Wimbledon Common, where elderly men and women exercised dogs and younger men and women exercised small children, then down steep Putney Hill. At the broad new bridge over the Thames, Rollison glanced towards the starting-post of the boat race, in which he had twice pulled a dark-blue blade, and caught Sal looking at him.

'Why *do* they call you the Toff?' she inquired.

'It's quite ridiculous,' said Rollison, accepting this concession meekly. 'My disreputable upbringing is really responsible. I used to like lounging about the East End, preferring the bar of a pub to a West End club, and the natives used to say "it's that toff again." Some turned the 't' into a capital, a newspaperman heard it and from then on I was doomed. Even strangers call me by it,' finished the Toff, as if sorrowfully.

'Oh, I know,' said Sal. 'They do at Scotland Yard, too.'

Rollison gulped.

'And who told you that?'

'Uncle Harry's had something to do with a recent Home Office Inquiry,' Sal said, 'and I went round Scotland Yard with him a few weeks ago. Your name cropped up. Uncle Harry was flabbergasted.'

Rollison shot her a swift and wary glance. Her dulcet tones might hide a barb.

'And what flabbergasted Uncle Harry?'

'They didn't just *laugh* at you,' said Sal, so calmly that it was impossible to believe that she was deliberately taking a rise out of him. 'They took you quite seriously. There was a Superintendent Rice or Brice or—'

'Grice.'

'That's it. He said that you could be brilliant.'

'At which stage,' said Rollison, coldly, 'I presume that Uncle Harry threw a fit.'

'Oh, no, he just laughed and said he couldn't believe it, you must show them a very different side from the side you show your relatives. Do you dislike your relatives so much?'

She was relaxed but not smiling. Soon they would return to the subject of Micky and the disappearing wooden ball and Micky's wilfully erratic aim but, for the moment, Sal was intent on making Rollison feel less annoyed with her; for Sal had not been stinted when intelligence had been handed round.

'Most of them,' agreed Rollison. 'I'm devoted to one and mildly attached to another.'

They had turned into New King's Road. There was little traffic. Rollison glanced at Sal again and was treated to a radiant smile. Sal had never looked lovelier, it was easy to imagine young men's hearts galloping fast at sight of her.

'You can be *so* charming,' she said. 'Who *are* you devoted to?'

'Be ready for a shock,' said Rollison and hid a smile, pretending that he was finding driving difficult. 'Old Glory.'

'Old Glory!' gasped Sal. 'That old battleaxe who—' She sat back in her seat. 'You're not serious.'

'I am wholly serious.'

'I don't think I shall ever be able to understand you,' said Sal, shaking her head. 'I really don't. I should have thought that Lady Gloria was so strait-laced you'd hate her. She doesn't *approve* of you, does she?'

Rollison grinned. 'We get along.'

'I suppose,' said Sal, and showed one of her many bursts of shrewdness, 'she didn't disapprove of you being a detective for a living but most of the other members of the family think it's beyond the pale, don't they? While you were just an amateur they could ride it but now you get *paid* for detecting, well, really, it's below the belt.'

She mimicked a particularly noisome cousin to perfection.

'You know our relatives well,' agreed Rollison.

'They're a stuffy lot, mostly,' said Sal off-handedly, 'but honestly I can't understand you liking Lady Gloria. She always looks at me through that lorgnette of hers as if I'm something that crawled out of cheese. I don't think she's ever said more than an aloof hallo to me.'

'I remember the last time you met,' said Rollison solemnly. 'There were seventy-nine members of the family, near and far, most of them women. You had the lowest plunge neckline of them all. Old Glory was in full cry to call attention to it and to ask you to go and put on a modesty vest.'

Sal breathed, 'No!' and turned bright pink.

'Yes,' affirmed Rollison and noted the blush and warmed towards this Sal.

He had known very little about her until the previous day when she had brought her troubles to him; he was beginning to think that there was much to be said in her favour, although his earlier information had not been.

'Who stopped her?' Sal demanded.

'I did.'

'Why?'

'Personally,' said Rollison, sparing a moment to ogle Sal, 'I like plunge necklines when the girl is—'

'Pig!' snorted Sal and stared ahead of her.

Her hair was almost black—rich, wavy, thick, setting off her creamy complexion beautifully. She was twenty-one and a bit. At moments Rollison thought that she should have been red-haired, to match her flashing temper and her imperiousness; but that was mostly due to the indulgence of Uncle Harry, her guardian. She had been parentless for fifteen years. Uncle Harry was a highly placed permanent official at the Home Office which explained his part in an official inquiry into matters of grave moment to Scotland Yard. A week ago he had come to Rollison, a worried man, saying that he did not know for certain but he believed Sal was mixing with bad company. Two or three of her friends were taking dope in the form of cocaine. He didn't think Sal was but he believed that she was worried. Would he, Rollison, prove that even far-removed blood was thicker than water and find out what was what?

A few days after this, Sal had come to plead for Rollison's help; that proved that she was worried.

She was very rich.

Now they were weaving in and out of the London traffic. Soon they would reach Hyde Park and Rollison would turn off towards the purlieus of Mayfair and Gresham Terrace where he lived.

'Rolly,' Sal began again, aloofly.

'Yes, Cousin Sal.'

She laughed, as swiftly and spontaneously as, a while before, she had spat at him.

'Rolly, stop fooling, *please*! I always knew we were cousins but I never knew much about you, except what most of the others said and that wasn't ever to your credit. *Did* you lose your fortune by gambling and riotous living and making absurdly generous gifts trying to reform criminals in the East End?'

'Yes,' said Rollison firmly, 'and no. You ask Aunt Glory next time you meet her, you'll find that she's human when she starts talking about the rest of the family and me. Sal, I have a living to make. There are several jobs waiting, Jolly always sees to that. But I can't handle two at once and do both justice. How seriously are you worried about Micky? Do you really think he's being blackmailed?'

Sal stared straight ahead of her. Traffic, very thick now, was smelly and noisy and went in sudden spurts. Traffic signals looked like the disembodied eyes of giants stuck on blackened totem poles. Rollison turned into Park Lane then turned right, weaved through gracious stately squares with smooth lawns and trees in the middle; through narrow streets lined with houses of the late and early Georgian periods, all beautifully kept, and came suddenly to Gresham Terrace, which was early Victorian and ugly. His flat, 22g, was at the top floor of a house near the corner.

He pulled up outside it.

He wanted to know how seriously Sal was harassed.

'If you really want me to help,' he murmured, 'I'll gladly try. But not if you're going to tell me half a story and not all of it true. And not if you're going to fly off in a temper if I say something that doesn't please you. If Micky is being blackmailed, then he's done something he shouldn't. If you want me to find out what's on, I'll try—but it might be something you won't want to know about. What's it to be, Sal? The truth, no matter how ugly, or wool over your pretty eyes?'

She looked at him, turning her head; and her pretty eyes were very beautiful indeed.

'I don't know,' she said and he liked her for that moment of honesty. 'Take me home, Rolly, please. I'll tell you what I decide later and telephone you.'

'All right. What time—I'll make sure I'm in.'

'Oh—between nine and ten,' she promised.

Rollison started the engine again, let in the clutch and drove to

Marlborough Court, a massive block of flats near Park Lane, where Sal had an apartment which cost a fortune. He got out and opened the door for her and watched her walking towards the sumptuous entrance hall. Two commissionaires, be-medalled and be-ribboned as splendidly as Ruritanian generals, hurried to greet her and bowed; one went ahead to open all the doors.

Life had always been very easy for Sal Hardy.

The Palace of Mammon swallowed her up.

Rollison drove slowly and thoughtfully back to Gresham Terrace, W1, which was a good address but dingy by comparison with the Palace of Mammon. Thoughts drifted through his mind. Sal, her prettiness which could almost be called beauty, her fiery temperament, her moments of calmness and—her fear? He thought that she was afraid but had no idea why. It might be that she felt fear for her Micky.

But was there more? Uncle Harry was not one to panic, and he was anxious, too.

He had not mentioned Micky.

Rollison thought the red-haired man casual and nonchalant, picking a quarrel with the huckster with big hands then going off with a wooden ball in his pocket. Ridiculous? Some young men of sportive spirit did carry off souvenirs: ash-trays and tankards from pubs, for instance, or a wisp of nylon to tell a tall tale of imagined conquests.

Had Micky taken the ball as a souvenir?

Why had so many people sallied into the fracas, purposefully rather than with enjoyment? It hadn't been late enough in the day for them to be drunk. Why had they wanted to start a disturbance?

Rollison left his car in the street and walked up the flights of stone stairs. As he reached his landing, the door opened and Jolly, his man, appeared. One glance at Jolly was sufficient to convince the sceptical that the specie *manservant Britannicus* was not extinct. While he lived there would always be one gentleman's gentleman; and there were those who believed that he would live for ever.

He bowed.

'Good evening, sir,' he greeted. 'I am very glad that you have returned. Superintendent Grice has been on the telephone three times; he desires you to go to Scotland Yard immediately.' Jolly said all this as if it were beyond all bounds of possibility that Rollison would obey such a command. 'He did not...'

Behind him, the telephone bell rang again.

'That will probably be the Superintendent,' Jolly said with a long-suffering air.

If it is, tell him I'm on my way,' ordered Rollison.

But he did not hurry back to his car. He followed Jolly into the hall and then into the large living-room-cum-study-cum-office where the telephone bell was ringing.

CHAPTER THREE

Policeman

JOLLY LIFTED THE telephone and spoke gravely into it, saying that Mr Rollison had returned and was already on his way to Scotland Yard. Jolly kept moving his head as he spoke, as if to give the words emphasis; and Rollison watched, fascinated. For, from this angle, a glossy top-hat on a peg in the wall behind Jolly appeared at one moment to be on his head; and the next an inch above it.

In the top-hat was a bullet-hole, drilled vindictively while Rollison's head had been graced by the hat.

'Thank you, sir,' Jolly said into the telephone. 'Goodbye.'

He rang off.

The hat resumed its proper position on the peg—just above a coiled hempen rope once used, folk swore, to hang a man and afterwards smuggled into the flat; the murderer had been very bad but might have been alive today had not Rollison, already famed as the Toff, taken a hand in his doom. This rope had a noose and it amused Rollison to show his favoured friends how it could tighten, choke and snap the life out of a man. It was fastened to an iron bracket, for better demonstration, and was the wall's showpiece. There were many other souvenirs, however, and it was Rollison's boast and Jolly's claim that every ornament on that wall had to do with murder and sudden death; even the poisons in their little glass phials.

'Do we know what Grice wants?' asked Rollison, mildly hopeful.

'I'm sorry, sir, but he gave no indication of any kind whatsoever.' It was Jolly's habit to leave no doubt when none was justified.

'Tone of voice?' asked Rollison, moving towards the desk. He began to fill his slim gold cigarette-case from a silver box, glancing at Jolly the while. Five-feet-six Jolly, clad in black and wearing a black cravat and butterfly collar, stood with his hands loosely by his sides. He had the glum face of a chronic dyspeptic and sad, strangely appealing brown eyes. His skin was pale and his face was deeply lined, as if he had once been fat but the flesh had withered and the skin shrunk.

'I was unable to deduce any inference from his tone of voice,' said

Jolly, 'but the frequency of the calls made it clear that the matter is believed to be urgent, sir. I doubt if the Superintendent would deal urgently with any *pleasant* matter.'

Rollison snapped the gold case.

'No,' he agreed. 'What have I done wrong lately?'

A glimmer of a smile dawned in Jolly's eyes.

'I cannot recall any serious misdemeanour,' he said reassuringly, 'nothing that would warrant arbitrary action on the part of the police, at all events.'

Then I shall go without fear and trembling,' declared Rollison and grinned. 'If Miss Hardy telephones, don't tell her where I am but say I won't be long. And if your little grey cells want exercise, present their compliments to a Mr Michael called Micky Ogilvie, aged twenty-five or thereabouts and an expert in judo. He's a useful boxer and he's played a lot of cricket, too. The only other start I can give you is that Miss Hardy is devoted to him at the moment.'

I will find out what I can, sir,' Jolly promised. 'It is true that two of Miss Hardy's friends have been undergoing a form of cure, sir—being addicted to drugs.'

'Snow?'

'Yes, sir, cocaine.'

So Uncle Harry had been right; Jolly would not make a mistake.

Rollison whistled softly to himself as he hurried down the stairs towards the street and the car and Scotland Yard. There were times to worry about the Yard but he did not think that this was one of them. Grice in a hurry meant a serious Grice but not necessarily a censorious one. Grice, in fact, was a man of great goodwill and much tolerance. More than anyone else at Scotland Yard, he looked benevolently upon the competitive detection of the Hon Richard Rollison. He liked the Toff. He even allowed himself to say, on special occasions, that he had much respect for the Toff's prowess. It was nice to be appreciated by the true professionals.

So Rollison whistled.

At Scotland Yard he was saluted by two men on duty at the gates and another where he parked his car and a sergeant and two myrmidons at the top of the stairs, in the reception hall. There he was told to "go straight on, Mr Grice was expecting him."

Grice had an office overlooking the Embankment. It was rush-hour and noisy; even the smell of petrol fumes came in at the open window where the pale green of plane-tree leaves fluttered in fits and starts. Barges moved with solemn sturdiness through the flat, untroubled Thames.

Grice was a big, brown man, over six feet tall, broad-shouldered, bony with a sallow complexion, a nose with a sharp bridge. There the skin was stretched tightly, showing almost white; everywhere else, he looked as if he had been sunning himself in Switzerland; it was his natural colour. He wore a loose-fitting brown suit and his brown hair, thinning and greying, had once reminded his wife of chestnuts fresh from their prickly husk.

He was in his shirt-sleeves and glanced up from his desk when Rollison went in, after a light tap.

'Oh,' he said. 'It's about time.' He pushed his chair back and went on without a smile, 'Since when have you been authorised to muscle in on our jobs?'

Rollison put his head on one side. He smiled. He crossed to the window and leaned against it, looking at Grice all the time.

'You don't mean to say you *work* in this place?'

That made Grice grin. It gave his face a pleasant expression, too. On the window side there was a nasty burn scar—the result of an explosion during a case in which he and Rollison had been working together. He was lucky that he had not been blinded.

'All right,' he said. 'What were you doing at the fair?'

'Oh, my Tipple! Showing a pretty cousin round,' said Rollison promptly, 'and giving her boy friend a once over in approved family fashion.'

'Really?'

'Yes.'

Grice said, 'So she's a cousin. Tipple said that she was as pretty as a picture and nicely ripe—'

Rollison winced.

'...and that if you were switching from the sophisticated type to her, you were on the downward path and we needn't lose any more sleep over you.'

'Until this moment,' said Rollison, 'I have always liked Tipple.'

'Cousin who?'

'Sal. Short for Ermyntrude, although you won't believe it,' said Rollison. 'Ermyntrude Dorothea Hardy who has a certain Uncle Harry Thomason—'

Grice almost jumped. 'No!'

'Who stole an hour from the call of duty to show his pet niece round Scotland Yard and introduce her to the exhibits,' said Rollison. 'I should transfer Tipple to a northern climate, if I were you.'

Grice had recovered and was nearly laughing.

'Well, I don't think that even you would take Sir Harry Thomason's niece out on a hunt through a den of vice, so I'll give you a clear bill. It's a pity, though, I hoped you'd know something—I thought that's why you were at Sharp's.'

'Sharp's?'

'The fair is owned by a family named Sharp,' said Grice, 'and most of the booths on it are run by his relatives. The family's almost as widespread and prolific as the Rollisons!' He relaxed completely, pushing a box of cigarettes across the desk, although he rarely smoked. 'I always have believed in the long arm of coincidence.'

'Never doubt it for a moment,' said Rollison. 'So there's a den of vice. It couldn't be the vice of blackmail, could it?'

Grice stiffened. He let the packet of cigarettes fall to the desk, leaned back in his chair and regarded Rollison without favour. All that seemed to Rollison a little overdone, as if Grice wanted him to feel that he'd scored a bull. The traffic roared on the Embankment and a tug hooted mournfully; overhead, a jet whined and whistled.

'Now stop fooling,' Grice said, in a sharper voice. 'Why did you go to the fair?'

'Uncle Harry's niece Sal asked me to take her. She has a boyfriend who, she says, is being blackmailed. She knows he goes to the fair quite often—it's usually on the outskirts of London. She had an idea that her boyfriend paid his dues there and knew he was going this afternoon. She asked me to go along with her, so that I could meet her Micky by accident. Michael called Micky Ogilvie,' Rollison went on, enthusiastically. 'We saw him but he got into trouble with a coconut shy and didn't stay to say hallo. Please, sir, I've told you everything.'

Grice grunted. 'I hope you have.' He frowned and began to tap the desk. Rollison took out his own cigarette-case, lit a cigarette and studied the detective.

'So you've an angle,' Grice said at last.

Rollison waited, patiently.

'Listen, Rolly,' said Grice and hitched his chair nearer to the desk. 'We've had several complaints about Sharp's. Three men have been robbed on the fairground and each lost big sums. Don't tell me that they shouldn't carry a lot of money about with them; that's their business and we have to protect fools. Two women have had expensive rings taken, too. There's been a lot of bag-snatching, dipping and the usual stuff. Pickpockets work all fairgrounds a lot but we've never known so many complaints as we've had about Sharp's this year. It's big and it's popular and the booths give good value. They get an unusually high-income-group clientele because the circus is good, and that means that there's a lot of upper-middle-class money spent there. So we've been watching it. This last month, we've had two blackmail cases to handle and each of the victims reported paying the money over at Sharp's.'

Grice paused.

'Any particular spot?' asked Rollison, softly.

'At the coconut-shy booth.'

Rollison pursed his lips in what could have been a soundless whistle.

'One of the men being blackmailed was due to pay a hundred pounds this afternoon,' said Grice. 'That's why Tipple was there. But the money wasn't collected because the blackmailer's envoy didn't turn up.'

'That's a pity,' said Rollison and meant it. 'Tipple's wonderful in every way except that he looks just like a copper. The blackmailer was warned off, was he? How's the money collected?'

'The victim is told to go and ask for six shies,' said Grice, 'and someone else follows him and has three. The pair stand in front of the coconuts together then go off together—and the money changes hands. It's a different envoy every time. It could be someone attached to the fair but we've no proof of that. That's everything we know.'

'I wonder what held things up this afternoon?' mused Rollison, looking as if he were thinking deeply. 'What time was the victim's appointment?'

'Half-past four.'

'At about twenty-past four we had the fracas. Ho-ha-hum,' mused Rollison and drew deeply at his cigarette. 'And you're after the Sharp family, believing they know just what it's all about.'

'I wouldn't go that far yet,' Grice temporised. 'But if you have a reason for poking around on your own, you might pick up something that we can't. It isn't Tipple's fault, fairground people can smell a busy. I can't give you the names of the people being blackmailed but I can give you descriptions. Next time there's an appointment—'

'If they were scared off by Tipple there probably won't be any more appointments at the coconut shy,' reasoned Rollison, 'they'll fix another place. Still, we'll worry about that when we get to it. This Micky Ogilvie. He's a ginger-haired, natty little chap—'

Grice said, 'Yes, I know, Tipple told me about him. Useful with his fists.'

'Any complaint being lodged against him?'

Grice chuckled.

'Sir Harry's niece can breathe freely. Sharp doesn't want trouble and the man in charge of the coconuts doesn't want trouble and we don't want any trouble, because if it got to court it might scare off the people who are using the fair for collecting blackmail. Will you see what you can find out?'

'And tell you?'

'Naturally.'

'It depends,' said Rollison. 'It depends on whether Sal wants me to go on with it.' He was sworn to secrecy about Uncle Harry's patronage. 'I've two cases hanging fire, each of them worth fair money, and the British taxpayer doesn't approve of employing private eyes when it pays huge salaries to Scotland Yard and all the other boys and girls on the force. But if I do find anything, I'll pass it on.'

'Thanks,' said Grice, as if he meant it.

'But I'd like to ask one question.'

'What?'

'Why was it so urgent? Why telephone Jolly four times?'

Grice stood up, twisted round for his coat and began to put it on.

'Oh, that,' he said. 'I wanted to catch you while you were hot on the fairground job and I thought it would make you get a move on if you had a guilty conscience.'

Rollison regarded him with acute disfavour.

'I ought to warn you about one thing,' Grice went on, breezily oblivious of that. 'If you start checking on the Sharp family, you'll soon come up against Leah Sharp. She's a daughter of the old man, Jonah, and helps to run the show. Some say she really runs it. Bit of a gypsy in her, she's as fiery as they come and has she a reputation!' Grice grinned. 'She's supposed to be dangerous to any man who gets within ten yards of her. But a beauty! Be careful of Leah Sharp.'

'You intrigue me,' said Rollison coldly.

'That's what I want to do,' beamed Grice.

On his way through the wide, bleak corridors of Scotland Yard, Rollison did not whistle and those who saw him twice were surprised by his expression. In fact, he was extremely thoughtful. Grice almost certainly knew more than he had said: Grice, in fact, was convinced that the fair-owners were a bad lot but could not get evidence against them. He wanted evidence, badly.

Sal was sweet.

Sal's boy friend had flung a glove, in a manner of speaking, into the fairground ring. He might get himself in nasty trouble. That did not worry the Toff at all for he believed that Michael called Micky Ogilvie was capable of looking after himself; but he might get Sal into a spot which was a vastly different matter.

Also, Sal was wealthy.

If her boyfriend were being blackmailed, it could be that he wasn't nice to know.

Rollison drove through the thinning evening traffic, dwelling upon all these things and reflecting that he was getting hungry. It was a night for dining-in and Jolly was masterly in the kitchen. The ideal would be a *tête-à-tête* with Sal and a frank talk about her feeling towards Micky and what she knew or suspected. Would she want him, Rollison, to go on? Or would she be frightened in case he discovered things that would reflect badly on Micky?

That was anyone's guess.

Jolly did not open the door this time. Rollison went to the tiny kitchen and paused on the threshold. There is a smell of roasting duck which can drive all senses but hunger away; and this roast duck was superb.

Jolly, slightly red in the face, turned round from the oven in his carpenter's apron.

'In fifteen minutes, sir.'

'Good. Any messages?'

'No, sir, none at all.'

'Oh,' said Rollison. 'That's a pity.'

He washed; had a pink gin; did justice to the roast duck, which was everything the smell had promised; he relished a Spanish red wine, savoured a brandy which was almost hallowed and all the time kept an ear cocked for the telephone.

Sal did not call him.

At half-past ten, when Jolly had gone to bed, Rollison put down a book of high adventure, looked at the telephone, turned an eye towards the death mask of a really lovely woman—who had been murdered by an artist who had blackmailed her. He disliked that association of ideas, jumped up and dialled Sal's number.

There was no reply.

He tried twice more and was not answered. That worried him for Sal had a maid, a country-bred maid trained in loyalty and absolutely reliable. Why didn't the maid answer?

At eleven, he poked his nose into Jolly's room.

'I'm going to Miss Hardy's,' he said. 'I hope I won't be long but stay awake, in case I need you, there's a hero.'

'I will, sir,' Jolly said.

Rollison, not quite knowing why he felt uneasy, went downstairs and walked briskly towards Marlborough Court which was only ten minutes' walk away from Gresham Terrace. The night was warmer than mid-afternoon had been. There were stars, shining upon the pale-grey roofs of London, and the chimney stacks carved black shapes in the star-peppered sky. London's noises were afar off, muffled by bricks and mortar and stifled by the great squares—but here and there were closer noises; of lovers, walking; or policemen, plodding; or cars passing, engines hushed as if knowing that their presence was an affront.

At Marlborough Court only one commissionaire with his splendid ribbons and medals was on duty. No, Miss Hardy hadn't come in, not since he'd been on, and her maid hadn't come out, either. Oh, they *always* left word at the office if the flat was empty, Miss Hardy's maid *never* forgot

'That's fine,' said Rollison and smiled upon him. 'I'll just go up and have a word with her.'

He hurried towards the waiting lift, his smile hiding an anxiety to which he could not put a name.

CHAPTER FOUR

The Flat

THE LIFT GATES closed behind Rollison without a sound. He stepped
on a puce-coloured carpet which muffled his footsteps; it was like
walking on down. He turned left, knowing that Sal's apartment was
in that direction: Number 27. He found it. The door was panelled
and gilded, there were gilt mirrors, some long, some wide; and mock
pillars also painted with gilt—too much ostentation by far; the Palace
of Mammon had a reputation for that.

The passage was wide.

Sal's was the middle door of three on the right-hand side.

Rollison rang the bell; there was no answer. He rang again. The
disquiet which filled him became an ominous thing, a kind of menace.

He had not felt like this until he had talked to Grice and realised
that Grice was really worried about the "den of vice" and the evil that
he believed was centred on, if not sponsored by, the owners of the
fair.

He rang for a third time and, receiving no answer, examined the
lock.

There are locks and locks, and those which have the best reputation
are not always the most secure. Some he could open without serious
difficulty, a thing which at times annoyed the police; others were too
intricate for him.

He thought he could manage this.

He used a knife with a variety of blades which would gladden the
heart of any conscientious burglar and it took him three minutes to
force the lock. In that time no sound came, no one approached; this
might have been a vast mausoleum, holding fast the dead in its gilt
opulence.

The door yielded.

The first thing that worried him was the light. It was on in the
hall—a square one with no windows but lights at the sides, above
imitation Dutch panel paintings with rich colouring. Sal or the maid
might have gone out leaving the light on but—

He did not let himself think beyond that.

He closed the door, very softly, and stood and listened. He heard nothing. Five red doors were in sight. He knew the flat, because an acquaintance of his lived in one in the same building, and he had learned that all were the same. He still walked on pile which was as soft as down. There was no sound at all.

Two doors were ajar. One, he knew, led to a passage and then the kitchen and, beyond, to the maid's bedroom. The other led to the drawing-room. He went in there and put the light on. Nothing here alarmed him. The furniture was large and expensive and in good taste; there were a few touches which looked like Sal and a photograph of Micky Ogilvie on a baby grand piano.

Micky was photogenic. His smile looked bright, there was an attractive air of nonchalance about him.

Rollison turned away and went towards the kitchen. The door stood ajar. He pushed and it didn't yield easily. He pushed harder, and something shifted—but was sluggish. He had to exert all his weight to get the door open wide enough to step through.

By then, his heart was thudding and fears had come hideous and close.

He switched on the light and looked down.

The maid's body was against the door and round her neck was a cord, tied so tightly that it was almost hidden in the flesh.

Rollison's fears became intelligible now, easier to face because they were known.

He bent over the girl but did not think there was any chance that she was alive. Her pulse was still, her wrist cool. She was a nice-looking plump girl, still wearing her black dress and little white apron and frilly cap. Trained in loyalty, he remembered.

He looked in all the other rooms; no one else was here.

With slow, deliberate movements, he telephoned Scotland Yard.

Then he called Grice, at Grice's flat, explained and added:

'Put a call out for Sal Hardy, Bill, I'm scared for her. Find her.'

Grice said, 'We'll find her. But what else do you know? What made you go there? Stay there until I arrive.'

'Find Sal, Bill,' Rollison said. 'The living are more important than the dead, even to policemen.'

He rang off.

Yard men would be here within a few minutes; or a patrol car might arrive first. The monied privacy of the Palace of Mammon would be invaded, the police would take over. He moved away from the body, squeezed himself back into the hall then went into the bedroom.

It was chaos; drawers emptied, pictures askew, the safe behind one of them opened—a combination safe in a thick wall. Rollison stepped across to it. He didn't know how much money and jewellery Sal kept; probably a lot. The safe was empty except for a few papers.

Burglary? Yes, of course, but had the burglar killed the maid because she had caught him red-handed?

Rollison stood for a moment, looking about him, trying to see through the chaos. He could picture Sal's face and lovely eyes, could see her Micky's grin.

There was nothing here to help, unless the cord at the maid's neck.

He studied this closely then hurried out of the flat, leaving the door ajar. In the passage he heard the lift whining so he started down the stairs. The lift opened, men with deep voices spoke and one of them was the voice of Detective Inspector Tipple.

Rollison reached the ground floor, unseen.

Two uniformed policemen were already on duty there, the commissionaire was looking shaken and a girl wearing white-paper cuffs over her sleeves was gaping at the police. A whisper seemed to come from her lips:

'*Murder?*'

Rollison strode towards the uniformed men, a visiting-card in hand. He smiled broadly.

'I'm Rollison,' he said. 'Superintendent Grice will be here soon, he'll want to know that I've just left. Tell him, will you?'

He beamed again and went out; and an echo that sounded like 'the Toff' floated after him. Two police cars were in the street, a third was turning the corner. Rollison went briskly towards the opposite corner and luck was with him: a taxi passed with its sign lighted.

It swerved in at his hail.

'Chelsea Embankment,' he said, 'near Albert Bridge.'

'Right, sir.'

Rollison slammed the door, looked out of the rear window, made sure that no one was following him, sat back and relaxed; but it was not true relaxation. He had not been easy in mind from the moment he had realised that Sal was late in telephoning him. Now, fear was very close. Why should her maid be murdered, choked until the life was gone out of her?

A cord round Sal's lovely neck would be an ugly thing, a sin, a sacrilege.

Rollison smoked. Sal's Micky lived in River Place, off the Chelsea Embankment, and Sal might be there. At least he must make sure.

Traffic flashed by, neon signs of a dozen colours winked and raced, dimly lit streets slid by the cab. No one followed.

Sal had gone off, saying she would let him know, and there was no telling what had happened to her.

He lit another cigarette, although his mouth was dry. They sped along the Embankment, tyres murmuring, with a few lights reflected on the Thames' dark surface, a little traffic coming towards them. Then the taxi swung across the road.

'About here, sir?'

'Thanks.'

'Shall I wait?'

'No, thanks.' Yet it might be wise to have a cab handy.

'I'll change my mind,' Rollison said, 'but if I'm not out in twenty minutes, off you go.' He gave the man a pound and in the light of a street-lamp saw the tired eyes brighten.

'Look out for me,' Rollison added and walked briskly along the Embankment, studying the houses. Over each front door was a fanlight, on some of the fanlights numbers were painted.

He turned a corner into River Place.

Micky's flat was in the second house—Number 6.

Rollison went to the front door and tried it; it was locked.

He did not know which floor Micky Ogilvie's flat was on. There were lights on the ground floor and lights on the top. He did not hesitate for long but used the skeleton-key blade of his knife; this lock was easy.

He opened the door.

The passage was lighted, dimly. Rollison closed the door and stood, listening; the sound of radio music came. On the wall by his side were three wooden panels, each with a name printed on in black. *Third Floor. Michael Ogilvie.* The third floor was the top floor.

Rollison hurried up.

The stairs were carpeted and he kept close to the wall, making little sound. The top landing had a strip of carpet leading to the flat door, that was all. A light showed at a glass fanlight above the door and Rollison heard a murmur of voices. One was a man's, the other a woman's. It was difficult to say why he felt his senses sharpen, why the hoarse, throaty voice of the woman clutched and held his attention.

Rollison stood very still, to hear what the woman said.

CHAPTER FIVE

Fair Fight

FOR A MOMENT, the voices were loud and the words quite audible. Rollison caught them all.

'...mistakes, Red,' the woman said.

'Now have you ever heard of me making one?' the man asked.

'The higher the climb, the farther the fall,' retorted the woman, 'and who knows, someone might be waiting to push you.'

The man said, 'Would her name be Leah, now?'

There was silence; then footsteps; then, unexpectedly, the closing of a door. From downstairs there floated the faint sound of radio music but that was all. Man and woman had gone into one of the rooms of the flat.

Rollison studied the door and its lock with his expert's eye. It would take a long time to force it. He moved back and peered upwards. In the hush of quiet his heart raced with a sense of urgency and in firm hope that one of the two people here knew where Sal was—and why the maid had been murdered.

Everything he did was swift, decisive; those who did not know him would have said that his acts were ill-considered. How could they know the bewildering speed with which his mind so often worked?

The glass fanlight was in a hinged frame. Locked? On the floor below he had seen a chair. He went down, close to the wall, ghost-like. He reached the chair, hurried up with it and placed it by the side of the door. He stood on it and saw light coming clear round the edges of the fanlight; so it wasn't fastened. It opened inwards and he pushed it down as far as it would go. It wasn't far enough, a safety catch held it. He unhooked this and lowered the fanlight until it was flush with the top of the door. He hauled himself up towards the opening, making a rustling sound. Would they hear? He slid through, head first, wriggling, catching his clothes against the side. He put a hand on the inside handle of the door and rested all his weight on this and lowered himself with agonising care.

His feet bumped slightly on the carpet.

He got to his feet slowly, watching a door immediately in front of him. The sound of voices came but he could not hear the words.

He opened the front door, moved the chair back into shadows where it would not be noticed, closed the door and then the fanlight and moved towards the room from whence the voices came. He touched the handle and opened the door a fraction.

'...don't make any mistake,' the man was saying, 'you'll be very sorry if you try to make any trouble.' His voice was harsher, he no longer seemed to be laughing at the woman. 'Remember that, Leah.'

After a pause, the woman said, 'Tell me *why*?'

There was another pause; then the man spoke in a quiet voice and it seemed obvious that he meant what he said.

'There's no logic in it, Leah, don't you know that. But she means a world to me.'

The woman said softly, 'I hate her and all she stands for, Red. And to think that she made a fool of you.'

'Why make it harder for yourself?' the man asked, steadily. 'Why can't you see it's the end of the chapter and stop fighting? I don't want to hurt you, but—'

'So you don't want to hurt,' the woman cried. 'You crazy fool, you—'

'Just forget me, Leah,' Ogilvie said, persistently. 'That's all you have to do.'

There was a pause. Then:

'I won't ever forget you,' Leah answered softly. 'I won't forget you if I live to a thousand years. And you won't forget me, Red. I'll see you dead before you marry her.'

It was the moment to move.

Rollison slipped into a room which was in darkness and stood close to the open door. The door of the other room opened. Shadows appeared and footsteps sounded. The woman Leah appeared. Rollison could see only her back but something in her carriage and the lift of her head told of beauty. She wore a tight-fitting wine-red dress magnificently. Red-haired Michael called Micky Ogilvie moved behind her and past her and reached the door. He stood with his back to it. Rollison dared to watch, although if he glanced his way the man might see him.

'Leah,' Micky said, in a different tone, 'we don't want to part this way. I—'

'Get away, Red,' the woman said.

Ogilvie stared at her, as if hoping to see some sign of softening; but there was none. At last he shrugged and gave a quick, flashing smile but his heart wasn't in it. He opened the door for her and Leah Sharp went out.

Her footsteps sounded; faded.

Micky hesitated by the open door then suddenly slammed it so savagely that the pictures on the wall rattled. Rollison moved swiftly out of sight.

'Oh, to hell with her!' Micky growled.

He went into the other room and didn't close the door. Rollison moved into the hall. He heard the chink of glass, the gurgling of liquid; after a pause, Micky gasped, as a man might after taking a drink that was too long or too strong or both.

'Be damned to the lot of them!' Micky cried and his voice was thick with anger. 'I wish—'

The telephone bell rang.

There was a pause before he answered it and it rang several times. Then he said:

'Ogilvie speaking.'

He listened.

He caught his breath. 'No!' The word came out like a bullet. 'No, it can't—'

Rollison moved until he could see the man. Ogilvie stood in the far corner of the room, sideways to the door, telephone at his ear. He was rigid. His face had turned the creamy pallor that some red-haired people favour. He stared at the wall and his eyes seemed to burn.

'All right,' he said at last. 'I'll come.'

He put down the receiver slowly and Rollison backed away and hid again. After a pause, Micky began to move about. Would he come in here? Micky appeared, following his own shadow. He went straight towards the door, looking like a man who was carrying a burden too great to bear.

He went out.

Now the flat was wide open for searching, the stolen ball might be here; but Rollison waited until Micky was down the first flight of stairs, then followed. The light on the landing was dim but Rollison could see the other man's shadow. Micky still walked slowly, as if the burden were truly unbearable.

He went out into the street and closed that door quietly.

Rollison opened it and was only three yards behind. Micky went straight across the road, towards a car which was parked beneath a street-lamp. Rollison left the street door open, so as not to bang it, and walked briskly towards the corner, turned, and found his taxi still there.

'Good man,' he said to the driver. 'There's a car starting up round the corner. Keep it in sight for me, will you?' He got in.

The engine of Ogilvie's car roared.

The taxi moved slowly after it.

A few minutes later Rollison knew that it was heading south-west, towards Kingston.

The fairground was quiet. An engine beat dolefully, probably making electricity for the caravans and stalls. Here and there lights shone on the doors of gaily painted caravans, on big, yellow and red lorries, over the entrance of the circus tent; but the lights were dim. A few people moved about, shadowy figures making little noise. Animals grunted, too.

Micky Ogilvie pulled up in the road near the big tent, got out and slammed the door.

Rollison's taxi passed.

It seemed to Rollison that Ogilvie was suffering from a great shock, he wasn't thinking straight; he did not appear to notice the taxi. It turned a bend in the road until it was hidden from Micky by the big tent and the driver stopped, putting on his brakes slowly.

Shall I wait?'

'All night if needs be,' Rollison said, 'and it'll be worth it.' He got out. 'Don't slam the door.' He hurried towards the spot where Micky had gone on to the fairground. The stars and the few lamps shed enough light but at first he couldn't see the red-haired man. He heard new sounds: footsteps. A horse whinneyed. A man began to strum a banjo, breaking the quiet unexpectedly; another began to hum. Rollison passed a caravan where the party was on and almost ran into Ogilvie.

Micky hardly noticed him; it was too dark for anyone to see that he was no fairground worker.

Micky went on as if he knew exactly where he was going.

Rollison kept twenty yards behind, watching closely, stepping high when he saw Micky step over cables and tent pegs and oddments on the ground. Micky passed most of the lorries and caravans. Some way ahead, apart from and almost aloof from the rest, were three or four caravans and two private cars, all shown by the light of a single electric lamp hitched to a tall pole.

Micky headed for this light.

Rollison, well behind him, heard a different sound, saw a different figure—a shadowy one, creeping from the cover of a lorry. Then he saw others. Suddenly the night seemed full of creeping shadows; of men, moving towards Micky. They were approaching him from three sides—only the little cluster of caravans and cars in front held safety.

Something glinted in a hand; steel.

'*Micky!*' shouted Rollison. '*Careful!*'

He moved as he yelled and the night sprang to life. The creeping men rushed, two of them at Micky, two at Rollison. Rollison saw Micky turn and saw another glint before men were upon him. He took a blow on the shoulder which hurt, rocked one man with a punch to the chin, felt a toe-cap brush his shin, drove his elbow into a yielding stomach. At the same moment he felt a buffet on the side of his head which sent him reeling. For a few seconds time was forgotten, he was in the middle of a whirlwind. The gusty breathing of fighting men, thuds as some fell, the shouting of others, footsteps, bright beams of light, were all part of the wild night.

Then, suddenly, a deep voice roared out and the whirlwind passed. Rollison was standing with his back to a lorry, hat gone, tie pulled out, collar ripped, coat awry and his mouth feeling puffy. Several men and two women were staring at him.

'Who the hell's this?' a man demanded gruffly and a torch beam shone dazzlingly into Rollison's eyes.

'Less shouting, Jake,' an older man said. It was the voice which had quelled the fight.

'At this stage,' said Rollison, 'the hero turned tail and fled.

Where's Ogilvie?' He put a hand up to keep the torch light out of his eyes and looked at another group of men. One was bending down.

'What do you know about Red?' demanded the man named Jake.

'Friend of yours?'

'Friend of a friend.'

'Jake,' began the older man.

'Leave this to me, father,' said Jake and glowered at Rollison. 'Who are you and what are you doing here?'

'I followed Micky,' Rollison said truthfully. 'The man you seem to call Red. And he was just about here when the avalanche fell, so I shouted to warn him. Is he all right?' He remembered the knives. 'Or—'

'You come with me,' said the older man. 'No, Jake, stand aside.'

Rollison sensed the hostility of Jake and others but that didn't matter. The old man was the Boss and he offered no danger. Rollison followed his sturdy figure. They reached the other crowd, where one man was bending over something on the ground, and the gruff-voiced old man said:

'How's Red?'

'He'll do.' The bending man straightened up. 'Bit of a cut on the back of his hand, that's all, and knocked cold.' He lit a cigarette and added contemptuously, 'Leah can look after him.'

For the first time, Rollison became conscious of Leah.

She was standing with the men on the other side of Micky. The light was poor but she was almost cruelly handsome. Her face was set as she said, 'Bring him,' and then went towards one of the caravans. The door was open and light streamed out, bathing her beauty and her animal grace.

A man lifted Micky Ogilvie and carried him after Leah.

'Now we'll hear what you've got to say,' said the gruff-voiced man to Rollison. He was stocky rather than big, a barrel of a man. 'Come with me.'

Jake, much the same build but younger, growled, 'It's time he talked.'

'Some other time,' said Rollison. 'I'll be delighted.' He beamed at them both then leapt away and began to run. Men grabbed and missed. He caught his foot against a cable but kept his balance and raced on. Men ran after him but he had a ten-yard start and knew exactly where the taxi was. He reached the road and pounded the even surface then heard the cab's engine start up. He was in the back of the cab, which began to move fast, before Jake, his father and the others gave up the chase.

'Back where we came from?' asked the cabby through the open partition.

'And you can't go fast enough,' said Rollison fervently. He leaned back, straightening his coat and his collar, poking his fingers through his hair, mourning his lost hat. When his breathing was steady enough for him to enjoy a cigarette, he lit one.

Mick was safe enough with rejected, cast-off Leah looking after him. There were many who hated him but Leah and the older man would not let them harm him. Leah might threaten to kill him rather than let him marry Sal but would protect him fiercely from others.

And—his flat was empty. Inside there might be a wooden ball of the kind used in coconut shies. There might be other things, too, giving some reason why Micky had been lured from the flat to the fairground and there savagely attacked.

Had his assailants meant murder?

The maid had been murdered, hadn't she?

And Sal was still missing.

CHAPTER SIX

Hollow Find

ROLLISON FORCED THE lock of Micky's front door, stepped in and closed the door softly then put on the light. Everything in the house was as quiet as he hoped it would be. He moved towards the room where Micky and Leah had talked. The light was still on. A bottle of whisky, an empty glass and a soda syphon stood on a walnut cocktail cabinet. The room was pleasant enough and comfortably furnished with an unmistakable bachelor's look about it; there were no feminine touches. But over the fireplace there was a wide mirror and Rollison caught a glimpse of his bruised right eye and a slight cut at the corner of his lips.

'Too bad,' he said, 'Jolly won't like it.'

He turned out the light in the hall. If anyone came they wouldn't see a light from outside. Then he went straight to the telephone and dialled Scotland Yard.

Superintendent Grice, please?'

'He is out, can I help you?'

'This is Richard Rollison. Do you know if Miss Hardy's been found?'

'Hold on, please, I'll try to find out.'

He held on, glancing about the room. Sal's photograph, touched up in colours, was on top of a bookcase. She looked too lovely to be true. Her smile showed her dimples and her eyes seemed to laugh; she was so very young and her maid had been strangled.

On the seat of a large armchair was a woman's bright blue handbag, the kind with a shoulder strap. Was it Leah's? Rollison hadn't had much time to think about Leah but he knew that she was magnificent to look at.

A man spoke. 'Mr Rollison?'

'This is Tipple. Mr Grice wants—'

'Have you found Miss Hardy?'

'No, sir. Mr Grice wants to see you.'

'At the Yard or Miss Hardy's flat?'

'Where are you now, sir?'

'Never mind, where shall I go?'

'Perhaps the Yard would be best,' Tipple said. Rollison could imagine him rubbing his cleft chin. 'Mr Grice says—'

'Tell him I'm looking forward to a cosy chat,' Rollison said with forced brightness, 'and also tell him that I'd like him to find Miss Hardy one of these fine days, if he could spare the time.'

He rang off and lit a cigarette; when he felt a little better, he picked up the bright blue shoulder bag. He looked inside and whistled very softly.

Lying with a compact, lipstick, a lace handkerchief, all the feminine oddments, was an automatic pistol.

He took it out cautiously.

It was loaded.

He put the gun back, made sure there was nothing else of interest in the bag, put it down and began to search in earnest. He went through this room swiftly; opening every drawer, moving books, shifting cushions, even looking in a flower vase and in the fireplace. A ball larger than a tennis ball wasn't easy to hide.

It wasn't in this room.

Rollison tried the next, a bedroom which obviously also served as study, for there was a desk, and also store-room because a cricket bag was against one wall, open; a bat was reared up against a corner, giving off a faint smell of linseed oil. A set of golf clubs in a battered leather bag and two tennis racquets were near it—and inside the bag were two cricket balls, one worn and badly battered.

Rollison lifted pads, gloves and another bat out of the bag, rummaged, found another ball and lifted it. It was as light as a feather, and had a different surface. He drew it out.

Here was the wooden ball from the coconut shy. He lifted and shook it but heard nothing. He examined it more closely and saw a thin line round the centre; that wasn't surprising, because the ball was in two halves. He held one half tight and twisted the other and it began to unscrew. Next moment, the two halves were in his hands.

The ball was empty.

He stared at the halves.

The insides were smoothly polished, they had been made on a machine. The ball was rather like a round Easter egg; papier maché with a good finish. He sniffed but smelt nothing. There was nothing to show what had been inside but he was quite sure that Micky Ogilvie had been after that ball, had started the fight for it and had got his way.

Rollison put it back where he had found it.

Searching for some unknown thing, something to help him to help Sal, was a different kettle of fish. What should he seek? He looked only for anything unusual but found nothing. Only one thing puzzled him: a receipt, dated the day before, for a month's rent of a caravan on a site called River Way, Williton, near Kingston, Surrey.

Williton was near the fair, he'd noticed a signpost.

He tucked the information into his memory and searched on. He was almost an expert and had acquired something of the precision, the speed and the thoroughness of the police.

There were three brief love letters from Sal; nice letters, the kind which could have been read in court without bringing a blush to anyone's cheeks; Sal *was* nice. Wasn't she? There was some money, in a small metal box which Ogilvie didn't even trouble to keep locked; apart from that Rollison found very little of value, except a gold dress watch kept in a cardboard box and wrapped in cotton-wool.

It was the flat of any young man; and the only things it talked of were a natural untidiness and a somewhat extravagant, eccentric taste in clothes. Micky Ogilvie possessed seven fancy waistcoats and Rollison broke into a grin when he discovered divers corduroy trousers and corduroy caps to match.

He found cheque books but no passbook sheets. Drawn cheques suggested that Ogilvie spent about twenty pounds a week; plenty but not extravagant for a modern young man about town.

Nothing suggested that he was being blackmailed.

The telephone bell rang.

Rollison started and glanced swiftly towards the door. It was after two o'clock, so this wasn't a casual call. The police? He moved towards the other room. The bell went on ringing. Could Micky's speaking voice be imitated? There was a curious lilt in it, just a hint of Irish brogue.

The caller would expect him to be in bed, too; would expect a voice heavy with sleep.

Rollison picked up the receiver, gave a realistic yawn and spoke in the middle of it.

'Hal—lo! Who's that?'

'Excuse me, Sir,' said Jolly, 'I hope I have not interrupted you at an inconvenient time but I have some urgent news.' He paused considerately and, when Rollison didn't answer, went on in a slightly less confident voice, 'That is Mr—er—Ar, sir, isn't it?'

'Mr Ar it is,' said Rollison, recovering but breathless. 'Don't ever shock me like that again, I thought it was the murderer.' A lesser man would have asked what had made Jolly call here; why Jolly had assumed "Mr Ar" was speaking. Rollison simply wondered who else might guess where he was and asked, 'What's the urgent news?'

'It is Miss Hardy, sir,' explained Jolly. 'She is here in a state of somewhat acute distress, not to mention an emotion which approximates hysteria. She—' There was a different sound, somewhere in Rollison's flat, and then Jolly completely forgot himself and gave vent to an explosive, 'Oh, damn the girl!' Then, 'I *beg* your pardon, sir—no, miss, really—excuse me, sir—'

'*Richard!*' cried Sal.

'So you've routed Jolly, have you?' said Rollison dryly. 'You'll probably live to regret it, he's tougher than he looks and has a memory as long as an elephant.'

'Don't keep talking to me about *elephants!*' screamed Sal.

'Sorry, no elephants,' said Rollison earnestly.

'And don't keep acting like a—like a *buffoon*, that's all you are, and I want, I need—' Sal's voice quivered, there was a long pause before she spoke again, much less fiercely. The words ran into one another in a way which Rollison could hardly understand. 'Rolly, everything's so terribly wrong, I need help so badly, please come at once, please come.'

'I'll come, just as soon as I can,' Rollison promised, 'but not there.' The police might call at his flat at any minute, Grice might be impatient. 'Not there—put Jolly on the line again.'

'I *must* see you, Rolly, it—it's desperate.'

'Stop being sorry for yourself! Put Jolly on.'

'All—all right.' Sal sniffed and then said so that Rollison could hear, 'He wants you again.'

Jolly was certainly a man to be admired. His voice held no hint of distress or resentment.

'Jolly speaking, sir.'

'Jolly, get her away. Take her to Lady Gloria, take her anywhere you like but away from the flat. Tell her I'm working on the case and that I'll join her as soon as I can. Don't tell her that the police might come and I want to talk to her before they can. Does she know her maid's dead?'

'She hasn't said so,' Jolly assured him and made a gulping sound. 'Is that a fact, sir?'

'Indubitably,' said Rollison. 'Get her away. Gag her if necessary.'

'At *once*, sir,' said Jolly. 'Goodbye, sir.'

He rang off.

Rollison pushed his fingers through his hair and stared at the wall. It would have been folly to talk over the telephone but he had to see Sal quickly. If she didn't know that the maid was dead, what was her trouble? Where had she been? Would Jolly be able to get her out of the flat before the police arrived? Grice would almost certainly go to Gresham Terrace.

Forget that...

He might never have another chance to search Ogilvie's flat, remember.

The only things he hadn't done were the obvious but elementary — like searching for loose floorboards and secret hiding places, examining the mattress, opening cushions and chair seats. If Micky Ogilvie had brought something valuable away in that wooden ball, would he have had time to hide it so thoroughly?

'Floorboard,' Rollison said, abruptly.

That meant shifting furniture, some of it heavy, and rolling back the carpets; but none was fitted and it was comparatively easy. His head began to ache, his eyes felt prickly, he was parched but kept on smoking. It was nearly three o'clock before he decided that there was nothing in the bedroom.

The furniture in the big living-room was easier to shift but the room was less likely as a hiding-place because the carpet was smaller. He shifted chairs, rolled the carpet, perspired, found no loose boards and none which was screwed down. There was nothing here, unless the chimney held a secret or the fireplace surround had a loose tile.

There was the kitchen, though.

He found nothing.

He gave up the search, reluctantly. He hadn't quite the same heart for it as when he had started for at least Sal was safe for the time being, even if the police would ask her a lot of awkward questions.

Who had killed her maid and why?

Rollison put everything shipshape; that didn't take long. When Michael called Micky Ogilvie came in, he would probably have too bad a headache to notice that anything was out of place.

Rollison stepped towards the hall door with the blue shoulder bag over his arm.

Then he heard a sound outside.

It wasn't loud; just a click, then the scraping of metal on metal. He stood quite still. He remembered that when he had been outside he hadn't seen any light.

Was this Ogilvie? If so, why had he come so quietly. Would anyone have let him leave the fairground on his own?

Rollison crept across the hall.

The sounds continued, metal on metal, very stealthy and cautious. A new sound came to Rollison's ears: that of soft breathing.

He almost held his breath.

The scraping sound stopped. He couldn't see the door but could imagine that the handle was turning. It creaked faintly. A light came on—the thin beam of a torch. The door opened wider and a man stepped through. All Rollison knew at first was that he was big; huge.

The torch beam moved round the hall, marking a white blob on the far wall which became smaller and elliptical as it went towards the corner. It drew nearer Rollison. He held his breath and kept motionless. He didn't like the size of the man; in any case, he had used a lot of reserves of energy and had no desire for another fight.

The light crept nearer.

Then a second light flashed on, much brighter; and the huge man showed up as a giant indeed.

Then:

'Stay where you are!' a man barked from behind him. 'We are police officers, and—'

The giant moved, swift and devastating as a great bear and disappeared from Rollison's sight.

CHAPTER SEVEN

Giant

'STOP HIM' a man shouted.

His voice ended in a scream, then came a thud and a groan. Rollison moved forward swiftly. The landing light was dazzling but he caught sight of the huge man bounding down the stairs. A Yard man was sliding down the wall, eyes rolling; another was falling down the stairs, pushed savagely by the giant. At the next landing the giant simply brushed this Yard man out of his way and made for the next flight. From below, a man with a deep but scared voice called: 'Stop there!'

'Stop a tornado,' muttered Rollison.

He could trip the giant by attacking from behind. He didn't. He turned up his coat collar and hid his face in it and sped past the two fallen Yard men; they would soon get help. The hall light was on. Two uniformed policemen stood between the giant and the front door. Rollison did not think that even four would have had a ghost of a chance. He only had a rear view but something in the giant's manner suggested primeval things; he was devastating; unstoppable. The policemen actually paled, one put his fists up defensively, the other drew his truncheon.

'Now—my man!' The first policeman squeaked.

The giant stood and looked at him, crouching, arms thrust forward. Looking down, Rollison could see his great packed shoulders, his massive bulk, his black hair with a tiny bald spot.

'Stop—where you are.' The policeman with the truncheon also drew his whistle. 'Nick, I—'

The giant gave a growling sound and jumped. The truncheon rose but didn't fall, the policeman rocked backwards and then toppled. The other, flayed by a swinging left arm, was flattened against the wall. He must have felt as if a car had knocked him down. The giant rushed out of the house while in the street a police whistle blew fiercely.

In the house the doors of the other flats opened. Shadows appeared and several scared people.

'*What's that?*'

'*Be careful, Charles.*'

'*Look, there's a man!*' That came from a woman, staring at the Yard man on the landing; he was trying to get up.

Rollison was halfway down the stairs.

The two policemen were out on their feet; neither made any attempt to stop him. The sight of that giant flinging them aside was never-to-be-forgotten; a jungle scene. Rollison slipped into the street where pounding footsteps showed an earnest attempt to follow the giant; but he did not think the man would be caught that night.

Rollison hurried to the corner.

The policeman in pursuit passed beneath a street-lamp and the blast of his whistle sounded clearly. A car came along and the headlights suddenly shone. They threw up the figure of the giant who darted across the road. For a moment, Rollison thought that he would run into the car. The car swerved, headlights did a strange dance, then the huge creature vanished into the shadows by the side of the river.

The policeman was still on this side of the road.

Rollison turned and hurried in the other direction.

Rollison whistled softly as he went up the last flight of stairs at Gresham Terrace, not because he felt like whistling but because, if Grice was waiting, he would be surprised by the absence of high spirits. There were times when the police had to be fooled and undoubtedly this was one of them.

The door opened as Rollison reached the landing.

Jolly appeared; and behind him, Grice.

Jolly, wearing a dressing-gown over his pyjamas, actually winked. That was all Rollison needed so as to rejoice that Sal wasn't here. He looked above his man to Grice whose lips were set severely; an accusing, unfriendly detective;

'Why, hallo, Bill,' said Rollison cheerfully. 'Hope you haven't been waiting long.'

'Where have you been?'

'Oh, out and about. I—'

'Where's Miss Hardy?' Grice demanded curtly.

During the time it had taken to exchange these frigid remarks, they had moved towards the living-room-cum-study. It may have been a trick of the lighting but the souvenirs of past man-hunts showed up vividly and were almost grisly; and now the hempen rope seemed to stretch down close to Grice's neck.

'Jolly,' said Rollison, 'coffee, please, hot and strong and a little lacing. I don't know, Bill.'

'Don't lie to me.'

'Cross my heart, I haven't seen Sal,' Rollison said and dropped into a chair. The cheerful approach had been a wrong one, after all, he should have come in dour and heavy-hearted; now he had to overcome the bad effect of the first impression. 'I wish to heaven I knew where to find her.'

'You know. Out with it.'

'Bill,' said Rollison, softly, 'I don't know. I went to see her and found her maid murdered and Sal flown.'

'You went after Miss Hardy and found her.'

'No, Bill.'

Grice said searchingly, 'Well, you know where she is.' Obviously he felt quite sure about that.

'If you were a lie-detector on two steel legs you couldn't make me tell you where Sal is. I don't know.' Rollison took out cigarettes and forced a smile; this was the moment for the 'let's be sensible and put a good face on it' attitude. 'And you haven't found her.'

'Not yet,' Grice said. Reluctantly, he seemed to accept Rollison's assurance. His voice was less harsh. 'Where have you been?'

'To the fairground,' Rollison said. 'Look at me!'

'Let's have the whole story.'

'Simple as can be,' said Rollison. 'After I called you I went to see Ogilvie. That's Sal's boyfriend. I thought she might have gone to see him, you know what young love is. He was leaving and I didn't have a chance to talk. I followed him to the fairground and, believe it or not, there he was waylaid by ruffians. To witness, my eye and my mouth. Ogilvie suffered a little more than I but he's not dead.' Rollison drew deeply on his cigarette. 'Or anything like it.'

Grice persisted, 'And after that?'

'I left Ogilvie being looked after by Leah Sharp.'

'So you've seen her,' Grice commented, as if with satisfaction.

'In a poor light only,' sighed Rollison, 'but she looks and sounds all you have promised me. Now for the confession. I went back to Ogilvie's flat with evil and felonious intent.' He grinned. 'I was going to have a look round. Someone else had the same idea. Do you know a man of six feet or so, with the proportions of a bear and the strength of an el—'

He cut 'elephant' short; could imagine Sal screaming at him not to keep talking about elephants.

'Why?' asked Grice, poker-faced.

'Such a colossus was at Ogilvie's. Your men were unlucky enough to catch up with him.'

'*Un*lucky?'

Rollison explained.

Grice said, very slowly, 'It sounds crazy enough to be true. I sent them to Ogilvie's place thinking Miss Hardy might be there.' He paused, then went on weightily, 'I'd like to know what you've left out. What did you find in Ogilvie's flat?'

Rollison's smile was sunny and serene. 'I didn't get far enough in!'

He glanced across at Jolly, who was bringing coffee on a silver tray and sandwiches on a salver. Jolly looked tired, as he so often did; he moved with great precision.

'Rolly,' Grice said, looking at the sandwiches as if he were hungry, 'don't make any mistakes about this job. I know I invited you to poke your nose in but I didn't give you authority to cock a snook at the law. We want to interview your cousin. I don't care who her Uncle Harry is, either. Her maid was found murdered in her flat and Miss Hardy wasn't there when we went, and she hasn't been back. She could have gone into hiding, and—'

Rollison said sharply, almost savagely, 'And she could be lying dead with a cord buried in her throat. Or she could be a prisoner, terrified, in fear of her life. Why don't you stop being a policeman? Find Sal.'

That outburst appeared to convince Grice that he did not know another thing. But he knew Grice. After they had drunk coffee and eaten sandwiches, Grice having more than his share, the Yard man left. He did not so much breathe fire and threats as leave behind an impression of stormy weather ahead. Jolly saw him out.

Jolly was gone for ten minutes.

Rollison was smoking and sitting and looking at the top-hat with the bullet hole when Jolly came back. He had finished inspecting two silken cords which had been taken, years ago, from the necks of a man and a girl.

Jolly came in quietly.

'How did you know where I was?' asked Rollison.

'I rang several places and arrived at Mr Ogilvie's flat by a process of elimination,' Jolly said. He went to the window and peered out cautiously. 'I can see no one in the street, sir.'

'Grice probably wants me to stick my neck out,' Rollison mused. 'I don't like it much, Jolly. I think that Grice knows much more than he says, that he hasn't been able to prise the case open and that he expects real trouble before it's over. So why not use the idiot Toff as an Aunt Sally? Where's Miss Hardy?'

'With Lady Gloria, sir.'

'Were you seen taking her?'

'No, sir, not to my knowledge.'

'How was she?'

Jolly said primly, 'You had some idea over the telephone, sir. I persuaded her to take a little brandy and introduced sufficient—ah— veronal to make sure that she will sleep soundly. She was already dozing when we reached Lady Gloria's hostel. I thought that best— for the police might go to the hostel, if they really wish to talk to Miss Hardy urgently. I thought that if she couldn't talk to anyone, it would be better.'

'Cunning as a fox,' said Rollison. 'Yes, I think so. Grice couldn't seriously think that Sal had anything to do with the maid's murder, could he?'

'The police,' said Jolly, judicially, 'have been known to acquire some quite peculiar ideas.'

Rollison stared at the little cords which had done their deadly work.

'Yes again. Did Miss Hardy tell you anything at all?'

'Nothing intelligible, sir.'

'She was just hysterical?'

'More accurately on the verge of hysteria.'

In the morning,' said Rollison thoughtfully, 'remind me to telephone Sir Harry Thomason and find out more about Miss Hardy's recent behaviour. Anything more on Ogilvie?'

'*Very* little, sir.' Jolly was regretful. 'I did manage to contact his Club, the *Ancient Sporting*, but all I gathered is that he plays a great deal of cricket and tennis in the summer, Rugby in the winter and golf all the year round. He gambles reasonably freely, sir, appears to be in no kind of difficulty. His home is in Ireland—Eire, I beg your pardon. The Dunoon Ogilvies.'

That meant that Jolly would pass Michael called Micky and sometimes called Red for any social register.

'And that's all?'

'He has a reputation for—ah—gallantry, sir,' said Jolly.

'A ladykiller, is he?' Rollison said heavily. 'I'm not surprised. Any details of his conquests?'

'There's been very little time to find out,' said Jolly but his tone of reproof suggested that Rollison would not have asked that question had he not been so tired. 'If I may be so bold, sir, I would advise some rest, after I have given a little attention to your eye and your lip. I don't think they will be disfiguring for any length of time. May I take a closer look, in the bathroom?'

Rollison got up and followed, meekly.

Sal was safe but hysterical. Grice was pretending to be hostile, actually allowing him a lot of rope. A grizzly bear of a man had been on the rampage—why had he gone to see Micky Ogilvie? Ogilvie had been attacked by men with knives, who might have meant murder, but also might have meant only to disfigure, to maim, or to frighten. Leah of the throaty, voluptuous voice was nursing him and—always remember—a plump country maid had been strangled.

Why?

Would Sal know? Was she frightened because of what had happened to the maid?

At nearly five o'clock, his bruises soothed by Jolly's ministrations, head aching, eyes very tired, Rollison dropped off to sleep. He had a feeling that he would not be allowed to sleep for long but that did not worry him; two or three hours would see him as lively as a man could wish and on his feet again.

He was granted six hours. He suspected but was not sure that most of these were due to Jolly who, on occasions, could surround him as a steel fence. But a little after eleven o'clock, Jolly appeared by the side of his bed, carrying a tea-tray and looking rather as if he had just left his tomb in the Pyramids of the elder Pharaohs.

Rollison struggled up.

'Who's dead?' he asked; and then remembered the maid, repented his flippancy and felt shadows gather.

'I don't think there has been any new development of great interest,' said Jolly. 'Lady Gloria is in the drawing room, however, and insists on seeing you.'

There was a pause. Then:

'That,' said the Toff, 'is an order.'

CHAPTER EIGHT

Lady Gloria

THE TOFF HAD a magnificent dressing-gown of royal blue silk shot with red and white roses. In fairness, it should be explained that this had been presented to him by a grateful Macclesfield client as a little bonus atop his fee. It was, in fact, a beautiful garment and he donned it before he left the security of his bedroom for the tempestuous world occupied by his oldest and his favourite aunt. Those—like Sal—who did not know Lady Gloria well, regarded her as a battle-axe or an old dragon; in fact, most were a little nervous of her. Even the Toff had known times when he had quaked before going into the presence. Now, he protected himself with a praiseworthy smile.

'Aunt Glory!' He moved swiftly towards her, placing his hands on her square, firm shoulders and planting a kiss on her leathery right cheek. Then he stood back. 'But you're looking wonderful!'

'And you,' said Lady Gloria, 'are looking remarkably like a gutter urchin after a squalid fracas in some malodorous public house.'

'And in a sunny temper, too!' marvelled Rollison. 'But sit down, Glory, and let me get you something.'

'Jolly is bringing coffee,' said Lady Gloria.

She moved, erect and graceful, dressed in the fashion of the late Edwardian age, high-breasted and magnificently corseted. Her gown was of bottle green; a filmy gauze, held high with bones, seemed to make it impossible for her to bend her neck. Hanging from her neck by a black silken cord was a gold-framed lorgnette. No one who knew her believed that she needed this for her eyes had a hawk-like keenness. She was a living hangover of a bygone age; and while she lived there would be always those who would regret that age's passing.

She sat down.

'Your eye will be black, blue, and purple before the day is out,' she announced, 'and your lips look very swollen already. Don't you think it is time that you stopped using your brawn and began to use your brains?'

'The happy thought,' murmured Rollison, sitting on the corner of his desk, 'being that I have some. Yes. But I got this through being a hero.'

'To whom?'

'Sal.'

'Ermyntrude,' said Lady Gloria, grimly, 'does not regard you as a hero.'

'But she doesn't know that I saved her life,' explained the Toff and offered cigarettes. 'Sorry I've run out of cork tipped.'

'I cannot bear paper sticking to my lips,' said Lady Gloria and from a pocket in the folds of her dress she produced a velvet bag; and from this a tiny cigarette-case, beautifully enamelled, some red-headed matches and, evident because they nearly fell out, a pair of scissors.

Rollison lit her cigarette.

'Thank you,' she said. 'Do you mean you think you've saved the life of this young man Ermyntrude is having the vapours about?'

'Mick called Michael *alias* Red.'

'I do wish you would stop using semi-technical terms such as *alias*,' said Lady Gloria, testily, 'I'm sure you only use them to impress. From what little I have been able to get the girl to say, it would have been better had you let him be murdered. Obviously he is being blackmailed and young men are not blackmailed unless they have committed some misdemeanour of which they have reason to be ashamed. You should know that.'

'No smoke without fire,' agreed Rollison and lit his cigarette. In spite of herself, Lady Gloria relaxed a little and smiled frostily. Jolly came in with coffee, put it down and departed. 'How is Sal?' asked Rollison.

'A very foolish, nervous young woman who should have had stricter handling all her life.'

'But in love,' murmured Rollison. 'Remember what it feels like, Glory. Remember the way the heart beats and the mind won't tick, how the emotions rule the intellect, even yours—why, even *mine*.'

'I almost wish you would fall in love and get married,' said his aunt with obvious sincerity. 'A sensible wife might knock some of the nonsense out of you. Yes, I think she is in love—and I even think she has some sense.' That was added almost grudgingly.

Rollison whistled. 'Sal's made a hit.'

'We shall now be serious,' declared Lady Gloria, picking up her coffee. She sipped. 'She is worried in case the young man Ogilvie proves to be a scoundrel. Do you think he is?'

'I only fear he might be.'

'Go on,' ordered Lady Gloria.

'There isn't much to go on about yet,' said Rollison, hugging one knee. 'Except that I think things will come to a head before long. Has she told you what happened to her last night and why she wanted to see me?'

Something in his manner made his aunt look at him very thoughtfully.

'Yes,' she said. 'She was telephoned by a man she doesn't know and told that if she wanted to save this Ogilvie person from the police, she must go straight to a certain place with fifty pounds in cash.'

Rollison didn't speak.

'She was foolish enough to go,' went on Lady Gloria. 'She took the money to Leicester Square Underground Station and paid it over to a youth by arrangement. This youth told her the police were at her flat, waiting for her. She telephoned her flat and was answered by a strange man. She wandered about in a panic, then eventually came to you.'

Rollison nodded, very slowly, trying to conjure up the picture of Sal wandering, frightened, alone.

'Then you wished her on to me,' went on Lady Gloria, 'but at least you had the courtesy to make sure that she slept during the night. Why were the police at her flat?'

'So she really doesn't know.'

'She *says* she doesn't,' said Lady Gloria. 'I really don't want my whole life disrupted by an hysterical young girl. Need the news upset her?'

Rollison said softly, 'Her maid was murdered.'

'Oh, dear,' said Lady Gloria and fiddled with her lorgnette. 'I suppose I feared some such disaster.'

'Why was Sal so jittery if she didn't know about it?' Rollison asked softly.

'She says that the youth frightened her. Oh, she has some guilty secret,' Lady Gloria said impatiently. 'In due course we shall know what. But that's not important now. I feel sure that she will lose her head completely when she discovers what has happened.'

Rollison stubbed out his cigarette, very slowly and deliberately.

'Don't you think so?' demanded Lady Gloria.

'Glory,' said Rollison, getting off the table; 'force the question and I'll say no, I don't think Sal will collapse under the strain. There's a lot of steel in our Sal. Once she realises that there's serious trouble, she'll be all right.' He flashed the smile which made him famous. 'So do you, at the bottom of that stony heart of yours.'

'Oh, she might be all right,' conceded Lady Gloria without enthusiasm. 'But I have no desire to give shelter to a young woman who is wanted by the police unless I am convinced that sheltering her will serve a useful purpose.'

Rollison had to chuckle.

'Bless your heart, you get more anti-social day by day!' He walked to the window. 'I'll slip over and see Sal and after that I hope she'll go to the police off her own bat. I don't think my friend Grice will be too difficult yet.'

'Very well,' said Lady Gloria. 'I'll tell her that you are coming and are doing all you can to help. What is this about her young man being attacked?'

'Don't tell Sal yet,' urged Rollison. 'It was an odd business. A whisper for your ears alone, Glory.' He stood close to her and there was a noticeable family likeness in the strength of the face and the cut of the lips and nose; and the clearness and steadiness of the eyes. 'Her Micky threw over a flamboyant fairground beauty for our Sal. A definite point in his favour. Don't assume he's a blackguard, yet.'

'If he isn't, find out and tell the child,' said Lady Gloria. 'She's eating her heart out in case he is.' She glared. 'And don't stand there grinning at me!'

Rollison, dressed, sat at his desk with the telephone at his ear and spoke to Grice.

'I know, Bill, I'm being difficult but I don't know enough to be helpful yet... As soon as I find Miss Hardy I'll turn her over to you, although she'll probably think I'm a traitor of traitors, family loyalty goes deep with us, you know.'

'Family pride goes deeper,' Grice said, showing his shrewdness. 'Don't protect Miss Hardy if you've any reason to believe that she—' He paused.

'My dear chap,' said Rollison, scandalised, 'she's the niece of a *very* high panjandrum in the Home Office. Be wise.'

'—that she's in a dirty business,' Grice went on as if there had been no interruption. 'You could get yourself into trouble trying to keep the family name clear of mud.'

'Nary a blot on the old escutcheon,' said Rollison inanely. 'Your base suspicions are unfounded. When are you going to come across and tell me what you're really thinking?'

Grice said, 'I think that if you're not careful you'll burn your fingers and I don't think that Miss Hardy is as much the butterfly type as you think. She could easily fool you and, if she does, you might find yourself in a nasty mess.'

'Listen,' urged Rollison. 'And—give. Please.'

'That's all I've got to say,' said Grice, 'except this.' He sounded as if he were enjoying himself. 'Don't spirit Miss Hardy away. We know she's at the Marigold Club under Lady Gloria Hurst's wing. It won't do her any harm to stay there for a while but she's to stay there.'

'Yes Bill,' Rollison said humbly. 'Tell me—!

'I'm too busy to listen to you any more,' said Grice, 'Goodbye.'

He was gruff; but there was never any doubt about his goodwill and there was no doubt about the seriousness of his warning. There was Sal's guilty secret and the police might know or guess what it was. There was a chance that she was simply shielding Ogilvie, of course; but that wouldn't make it easier for her if Grice really believed that she had killed her maid. Would he hold off, if he did?

Sal had such beautiful blue eyes, such a wonderful look of innocence, when she was in the right mood—yet she was so frightened that she was never in the right mood for two minutes at a time. She was at screaming point one minute, showing a prickly kind of calm the next. Fear for her Micky? Or fear for herself?

'Jolly,' said Rollison, putting the receiver down slowly, 'life's hard. You have to do the work of two men. We could use some help on the fairground and we need to know whether Micky and Leah have made up their differences. It probably depends on whether she's a capable nurse.' He smoothed his chin and Jolly, seeing the glint in his grey eyes and the set of his lips, knew that he was not only thinking at high pressure but was already several moves ahead of his words. He sounded almost absent-minded. 'Go and see Bill Ebbutt. Tell him I'd like one or two bruisers to go over to the fairground, all expenses paid. Also one or two reformed characters who will know which dips and con men are working the place—what's the park called?'

'Gibben's Field, sir.'

'Now if it were Gibbett what a pretty touch of irony,' observed Rollison. 'No, I am not as demented as I sound. If Ebbutt can get one or two men on the fair, it would greatly help. If there's a boxing booth it should be easy. You know the general run of what we need.'

'Yes, sir. What, in particular, is Mr Ebbutt to look for?'

'Leah Sharp, her lovers past and present, Micky the Red Ogilvie and a man looking like a polar bear who raided Micky's flat last night.' Rollison went to the desk and opened a drawer and took out a bright blue shoulder bag. 'Good quality, Jolly, if a bit flamboyant. Who should be surprised? The bear might have gone to get this because Leah left it behind; or he might have gone to get that coconut-shy ball.'

'Have you searched it, sir?' asked Jolly, prosily.

'Superficially. You could do much better. Turn everything out.' Rollison watched Jolly as he obeyed, maintaining a masterly deadpan as he brought out the gun.

Jolly put the gun down and picked up a gold-coloured metal lipstick container. He twisted it. The greasy red stick bobbed up; almost new, judging from the shape. Jolly twisted it back again and put it aside but Rollison moved and picked it up.

'A pretty little thing, a very pretty little thing, all pure gold unless I'm badly mistaken. What is the purpose of this pretty little thing?' He was oblivious of Jolly's almost scathing look as he twisted and turned and ran his thumbnail round the little grooves. 'The lipstick looks small for the length of the container, Jolly, but that may be—ah!'

There was a click.

The bottom of the lipstick case sprang open.

A sprinkling of white powder fell out.

CHAPTER NINE

White Powder

BOTH MEN STARED at the sprinkling of powder on Rollison's fingers, on his coat and, now, on the floor. Rollison had tipped the case up quickly; most of the powder was still inside.

They shot each other swift, understanding glances.

'Here we go,' Rollison said, in a voice which was hard and yet strangely hollow. He raised his left hand to his mouth and tasted the white powder gingerly. Now his face was quite expressionless except for his eyes; and his eyes stormed. 'Whether we want it or not, we've got it. The discovery of a secret.'

'*Cocaine*,' breathed Jolly.

'That's right,' said the Toff. 'Pure white snow. Now you have to do the work of three men, Jolly. Get this stuff analysed, make sure I'm right. Be very careful with it.'

'I will indeed,' Jolly said.

The Toff looked at him and smiled, his expression touched with affection.

'Did I ever tell you,' he said, 'that I think the word impeccable was coined for you? I'm going to see Miss Hardy.'

Sal's eyes were so bright and blue.

She was very intense, too; her lovely little body seemed to be screwed up, as if her nerves and her muscles were bunching together, making some unspoken protest against an unknown but fearsome threat. She was clear-skinned and without a blemish, her hair was just a dark curly mop. She was a dream for a young man in love.

'But I didn't *know*!' she cried. 'Even now I can't believe it, I just can't believe that Jessie is dead. *Murdered*. It doesn't make any sense, why should anyone do a thing like that?'

'It seems that they went to rob you,' Rollison said.

He watched her very closely. Lady Gloria, sitting on a couch and looking relaxed, was in fact just as sharp-eyed. She had been warned of the possible cause of Sal's excitability.

'But to *kill* Jessie—oh, it's awful, it's dreadful, it—'

'Sal,' said Rollison, very gently, 'you knew, didn't you?'

'No!' she cried tempestuously. 'No, it's not true, I didn't know, I've told you what happened. Oh, why won't you believe me?' Tears were spilling over in her eyes and her voice was shrill. 'I didn't know! Why don't you try to help instead of being so beastly?' She caught her breath and then swung round on Lady Gloria. 'It's *her* fault! She hates me, she's turned you against me!'

'Don't be ridiculous, child,' said Lady Gloria, coldly but without umbrage. 'Richard is trying to help. If you tell him the truth, he'll have much more chance.'

'But I've told him the truth!'

'Sal,' said Rollison, 'the youth told you that the police were at your flat, you say. Why were you frightened? Why didn't you go and find out why they were there?'

'I thought I knew,' she cried. 'Oh, Rolly, I've been such a fool. I— I've smoked a few reefers, cigarettes with cocaine in them. I know it was crazy! I—I had a few left over. I was afraid the police would find them.'

'I see,' said Rollison, very gently. 'Where did you get them from, Sal?'

'From a girl friend,' Sal said, almost sobbing. 'But, Rolly, last night Jessie was alive when I left. I swear it. It must have been about seven o'clock. I didn't wait for dinner. I was so agitated. The man who telephoned for the money said I'd go to prison if I didn't take it.'

'No friend, that man,' Rollison said.

Sal was living on her nerves, then, as a snow addict would. The sooner a doctor saw her, the better.

'All right, Sal,' he went on soothingly. 'I'll do all I can. Don't run away with the idea that Old Glory has a rod in pickle for you, she'll be happy to help.'

'She knows that I will,' chimed in Lady Gloria.

Sal's eyes brimmed over again.

'Oh, I know, I'm such a beast but I'm so frightened. It's like living in a nightmare. I love Micky so much and yet I'm afraid—'

She broke off, shivering, and would not say another word. Had a "girlfriend" supplied those cigarettes? Or her Micky?

Rollison left her with Lady Gloria, half-convinced that she was taking drugs. But she was a long way from being an incurable; a short, fierce fight would beat the craving.

Who had introduced her to the drug? And why?

She was wealthy, remember; she could sign a cheque for ten thousand pounds without making any difference in her daily spending. She would be a fine catch for Micky the Red, a fine enough catch to make him throw over the beautiful Leah.

She would be a fine catch for anyone.

If she were being blackmailed, for instance, she would be a regular source of income.

Lady Gloria would soothe her and get a doctor.

The Marigold Club was a kind of hostel run by Lady Gloria, who hated idleness and was full of good works. Its rooms were tenanted by young women who were in need. Rollison had taken physical wrecks there and seen them, a few months afterwards, well again in mind and body.

Rollison drove to Scotland Yard. The sergeant on duty in the hall told him that Grice was in. He was an elderly, understanding man who liked his little joke and knew that the Toff and the Super were close friends.

'I want to catch him having forty winks,' said Rollison conspiratorially, 'don't tell him I'm on the way.'

'Right you are, sir! But you'll have to get up early to catch the Super asleep!'

Rollison winked.

Grice's door was closed; there was no sound of voices, so he wasn't on the telephone. The Chief Inspector who shared the office might be there. Rollison did not tap but flung the door open. One glance told him that Grice was alone. Grice was so startled that he jerked his head back and banged his head on the wall. A little harder and Rollison would have been forced to commiserate. Instead, he glared.

'Who let you in?' demanded Grice.

'Listen, Bill,' growled Rollison. He kicked the door to with his feet and went forward, his expression glowering and his eyes flashing; he looked like this when he was putting the fear of gaol and the gallows into the hearts of evil men. 'I don't mind being played for a fool. I don't mind being the Yard's stooge. I don't even mind when you pull a fast one on me but I'm damned if I'll stand for this.'

Grice was shaken into being mild, almost apologetic.

'What's this all about, Rolly? I don't—'

'Why the hell didn't you tell me this was a drug racket?' The question hovered like a shadow. Once before, at mention of blackmail, Grice had shown exaggerated concern. Now his expression changed from one of bewildered remonstrance to astonishment; he gave the truth away completely. Rollison stood with both hands on his desk, leaning forward, that 'I-am-going-to-get-you-one-day' glint in his eyes. Grice fought to glare back. Rollison's expression gradually changed; he began to smile, then he smiled broadly and finally he beamed.

'Thanks, Bill,' he said.

'You sly devil!'

'Oh, naughty. Strong language in these hallowed precincts will not do. So it is a drug show.'

Grice tried to rescue himself.

'What makes you think so?'

Rollison put his head on one side, moved forward, took a cigarette from Grice's packet with a murmur of thanks, lit it and then sat down in the armchair, hitching up his trousers with great precision and concern. His smile faded.

Sal Hardy's smoked a few cigarettes she calls reefers but they might contain snow or morphia, not marihuana. Did you know?'

Grice drew a deep breath, then ran his fingers about his bony brown-skinned chin and said, 'I thought she might.'

'She says she stayed away from her flat because she was afraid you'd find them and she'd be for it.'

'Guilty conscience,' Grice said mildly.

'Someone's scared the wits out of her.'

'Someone killed her maid,' Grice remarked dryly. 'Where did she get the stuff from?'

'A girl friend.'

'Named?'

'Not yet.'

'Couldn't be a boy friend, could it?' asked Grice, too quietly to be sarcastic. 'Is she trying to shelter this Ogilvie?'

'Bill,' Rollison said, 'as I sit here, I don't know.'

'Rolly,' said Grice, 'as I sit here I don't know either. I do know there's a lot of snow about and we're after both the filthy stuff and the pedlars. A lot of girls from good families, like Miss Hardy, have become addicts. Some have gone too far for us to help. Hopeless cases. Someone is distributing. There was a rumour that snow was being handed out at Sharp's fairground.'

Rollison interrupted, '*Not* blackmail, Bill?'

'Small stuff only.'

'What about other crime at the fair?'

'A little. There always is. You were like a dog with two tails over a blackmail angle and who am I to take a tail away?' Grice was almost skittish. 'But our big worry is drugs.'

'So is Sal Hardy's and Uncle Harry's. Any indication that Ogilvie's in it?'

'No.'

'The Sharps—Leah, her father, Jake?'

'No.'

Rollison looked at Grice and wondered what he would say if he knew about the lipstick holder and its secret hoard. The time to tell had not yet come. There was dope—on a big scale or Grice wouldn't be so worried—and snippets of blackmail, frightened Sal, battered Ogilvie and vengeful Leah.

It would take some sorting out.

'Bill,' Rollison said, 'do you know what time Sal Hardy left her flat last night? Whether it was before or after the death of her maid?'

Grice said slowly, deliberately, 'No, I don't. If I knew she was there after the maid died, I'd pull her in. I'm checking. Don't do the wrong thing and spirit her away. I shall expect to find her at Lady Gloria's when I want her.'

'Yes, Superintendent,' said Rollison.

He went out, subdued of heart, restless, anxious. Uncle Harry would soon have to be told of progress or the lack of it; he was keeping remarkably quiet. Sal was his great worry and Sal was in a spot...

Rollison's club, the Carilon in Carlton House Terrace, was nearer than Gresham Terrace. He telephoned Micky Ogilvie's flat; there was no answer. He telephoned his own place. The "daily help" answered, a middle-aged and grey-haired woman with a nice face and nice temperament who might one day become Mrs Jolly. That was a constant reminder to the Toff that life could change very quickly.

'Mr Jolly's gone to the East End, sir,' she said. 'He asked me to tell you that your first diagnosis was quite right and said you'd know what he meant.'

'I do,' said Rollison. 'Thanks. Tell him I hope to call up or be home by one o'clock. If I'm seriously later, ask him to dig for the body in Gibbett's Park.'

'*Gibbett's?*'

'He'll know what I mean,' said the Toff. 'Goodbye.'

He rang off, had a quick lunch then walked briskly through the high, cool rooms of the club, his right hand in his pocket fingering the gold of Leah Sharp's lipstick.

He got into the Rolls-Bentley and headed for Kingston at speed.

CHAPTER TEN

Gibben's Field

THE FAIRGROUND PRESENTED a dismal sight. Here and there a man or a woman moved about, almost furtively, but the booths stood empty and drab. The colour and vitality that crowds and noise put into the fair was gone. No voices were raised. The generating plant beat its dreary note, a few animals made mournful sounds.

Rollison drove towards the group of better caravans which proved to be in a corner of the huge field, a little higher than the rest. He passed the big Circus tent. An elephant appeared, swinging its trunk; then another and another followed and behind them walked a diminutive boy with a coffee-coloured skin and a bright green turban. He gave Rollison a dazzling, almost cheeky smile, as Rollison stopped for the elephants to pass.

There were seven.

They moved on with their majestic stateliness and Rollison eased off the clutch. Then a sound of hammering broke the quiet and he looked round. Just in sight was another square canvas tent with a huge canvas sign, reading:

IVAN THE TERRIBLE
CHALLENGES ALL COMERS TO A MATCH
OF BOXING OR WRESTLING
£5 to all who last ONE round
£50 to all who can defeat IVAN

Near this, a man was hammering at some tent pegs. "Man" was one word. A sober spectator could have been forgiven for thinking "bear" if he caught sight of this creature in a zoo or in hill country overseas. He was huge, vastly over six feet, and broad in proportion. His body, naked to the waist, was like a barrel, his enormous chest was made almost frightening by the great covering mat of wiry black hair. His arms were colossal and, as he wielded the wooden hammer, his muscles bulged as if the very skin would burst.

No one could doubt that this was Ivan the Terrible.

And the police hadn't got round to him yet. Or else they were watching and waiting.

Rollison stopped. Ivan finished his hammering and looked round. He did not smile. He had a large, waving moustache, as black as his great mane of hair and the mat on his chest. In an alarming way he was a handsome creature; his big features were regular, there was aggressive strength in the expression as well as in the great body. His eyes beneath jutting dark eyebrows were a light brown; tawny, unexpected—making him even more of a puzzle.

The Toff smiled upon him. 'Good morning.'

Morning,' said Ivan, in a low-pitched growl. He had a marked accent.

'Lovely morning, isn't it?' asked Rollison brightly. 'I'm looking for Miss Leah Sharp. Can you tell me where to find her?'

Ivan scowled.

He was too big, too massive, too real to be true; but he was true enough. His scowl declared disapproval, suspicion and ill-will and all of Rollison's brightness could not dispel these facts. As he moved, great muscles rippled on shoulders, arms, chest and torso. Here was a candidate for the Original Hairy Man, fit for any Hollywood jungle film.

'Why do you want Miss Sharp?' The "why" was almost but not quite "vy;" and the "want," "vant."

'I've a message for a friend of hers,' said the Toff. 'From Mr Ogilvie.' He beamed. 'And this.' He held up the bright blue bag.

Ivan's brows met together in a mighty frown; he looked as if he were going to throw himself forward and grab the bag. He did not.

'Where did you get that?' The "that" was nearly "dat," and the guttural growl was oddly attractive; and right for him. It was like meeting a bear who had conquered the art of speaking.

'Oh, places,' said Rollison. 'Do you mind telling me where she is?'

Ivan still regarded him with glowering suspicion. Two other people had now appeared and stood and stared—one admiring the Rolls-Bentley, the other apparently relishing the tussle between these two men. There was Rollison, lean and supple as a panther; and Ivan, more bear than man.

It was unbelievable that anyone could have such great physical strength and be a quick thinker, too. So Rollison was patient. He missed nothing that there was to see in Ivan and quickly came to the conclusion that he would not like to try to win either the five or the fifty pounds in combat. He remembered the way in which hefty Scotland Yard officers had been flung aside and smashed against the wall; and that could happen again. He wouldn't like to be with the police who eventually came to try to arrest Ivan.

They were bound to, sooner or later.

The great creature made up his mind at last. He raised a hand and pointed towards the isolated group of caravans.

'There,' he said. 'The green one.'

'Oh, good!' said the Toff gratefully. 'Thanks a lot.' He touched his forehead with the bright blue bag and started off.

Ivan and the others watched him but soon he noticed that Ivan disappeared. That was not for long. By the time that Rollison was half-way between the fighting booth, Ivan had appeared again, this time alone. He had put on a coat and was striding in the wake of the car.

Rollison studied the exclusive caravans which were obviously those used by the Sharp family. He had learned a little more about the fair. There was true Romany blood in the Sharps but it had been so diluted that most gypsy traits were gone; and some thought that a bad thing. The Sharps were aristocrats of the travelling-fair business and in their own domain they were like dictators, living aloof from their subjects. Yet there was much to be said for them. The patriarch, seventy-year-old Jonah Sharp, had three sons and two daughters. Except for Leah, all of these were married and had families; and all were in the business. Jake was the eldest. By all accounts, though, Leah and not Jake was second in-command to old Jonah.

Leah's was the vivid green caravan, beautifully made and brightly painted, on pneumatic-tyred wheels and meant to be drawn by a car, not by horses. Yet it was designed in true Romany style, there were little flowered curtains at the windows and a single metal chimney rose from the curved roof, giving off a steady stream of pale grey smoke. Beyond, the sky was beautiful with only a few white clouds to disturb the gentle blue.

Rollison pulled up just behind the caravan.

The door, at the back, was like a horse-box door; and the top section was open. He could see burnished brasses hanging on one wall.

'Anyone home?' he called.

There was a sharp sound inside. Then a woman, Leah, said, 'Who's that?'

'Better find out.' That was Michael called Micky the Red. The slight brogue was in the voice; and also the slight air of insolence.

Rollison got out of his car.

The woman appeared.

She wore a scarlet cloth twisted round her head, turban fashion, and a scarlet jumper, so tight-fitting that every hint of a curve in her wonderful figure was shown triumphantly. The jumper was high at the neck and the sleeves stopped just above the elbows. She had fine, browned arms, nicely shaped hands with scarlet nail-polish; and somehow it was surprising to see her holding a spoon with something white and doughy on the end of it.

The sun shone upon her lovely face, throwing up each feature in vivid relief. Most women would have suffered grievously under those searching rays but not Leah Sharp. Hers was a beauty which could bear any light. Her eyes were dark blue and hinted at depths, like the great depths of the blue sea. Her complexion had the creamy perfection of a peach just taken from the tree and her lips...

'My, *my*,' marvelled the Toff, in silent wonder.

She looked at him without speaking, leaning against the lower part of the door, the doughy stuff dripping from the spoon. Her air was casual and yet superbly confident. Whatever had happened at Micky's flat was forgotten for Rollison had one distinct impression; that she was a happy woman.

Not like Sal.

'Good morning,' said the Toff, in his deepest and most impressive voice. 'Have I the pleasure of speaking to Miss Leah Sharp?'

Her lips parted in an ironic smile, as if she knew exactly what effect she had on him.

Micky called out for her.

'You have and it's your own good luck!' A pause. 'Who would it be, Leah?'

Rollison moved towards Leah. She watched him closely, as if beginning to doubt whether she had bowled him over so completely after all. Near them, only fifty yards away, was Ivan the Terrible, his massive torso hidden by the old coat; and behind her was Micky the Red, still out of sight.

'Well, who would it be?' asked Leah. That deep voice, throaty, warm, hinting of forbidden things—was that just a quirk of the mind? Could there be such a thing as a sex-laden voice?

'A very good friend of the pair of yez,' declared the Toff, in an Irish brogue so deep and real that it startled her. 'Look what I've brought yez, now!'

He drew the bag from beneath his coat and held it up.

At the sound of his voice, Leah had started to smile and he thought again that she was a happy woman; he went farther, it was almost as if she knew some secret of happiness. It was part of her; an animal contentment—she was as a great cat might be, some jungle beast which had killed its prey and fed well on raw flesh and was satisfied. Her lipstick, much too bright for her colouring, might be the prey's blood; dripping.

When she saw the bag, she caught her breath, her teeth showed, her eyes took on a fiery light.

Ivan was much nearer now; Rollison could hear his footsteps. There was no movement inside the caravan and there was only the hushed sound of Leah's breathing. She looked into Rollison's eyes as if she were trying to divine the truth of what he had discovered.

Then Micky called, 'What the devil is it? Here, I'll come and see.'

She turned. 'You stay there!'

'I'll be damned if I will!' There were creaking sounds and Leah turned away and disappeared. The creaking continued, Micky expostulated but sounded as if he were getting the worst of whatever was happening. Ivan was *very* close.

Rollison went near enough to look inside.

It was just the one room with a narrow bed stretched across the far end. Leah was forcing Micky the Red down on to it, pressing one hand against his chest. He was dressed in shirt and trousers and his right foot was like an enormous turnip, being bandaged round and round and round.

Suddenly, Leah took her hand away from his chest, clutched his hair, and thrust him back.

'Ouch!' he gasped and stopped struggling.

'Now do as you're told,' said Leah, quite calmly; but when she turned round, Rollison knew that the calmness was only in her voice, her thoughts were in chaos.

Yet she had the habit of calmness; of self-control. She was completely self-possessed and it was easy to believe that whatever task she set herself she would do it superlatively well. If it were collecting blackmail or if it were spreading drugs to rot the minds of men and women, she would do it with a single-heartedness which it would be hard to beat.

'May I come in?' asked the Toff. He rested the blue bag against the top half of the door, so that she could see it.

Ivan had stopped and his breath touched the back of Rollison's neck.

Leah looked past Rollison towards the giant, as if sending him a message; and in that moment, Rollison felt afraid. He did not like the feeling and was not used to it. But this vast creature behind him could crush him in those great arms; could squeeze the life out of him, could crack his bones until they splintered.

'Give me the bag,' said Leah, quietly.

Rollison moved his head and maintained his smile and handed her the bag. She opened it. Micky Ogilvie stared from the bed, leaning on one elbow. The tension could not have been greater. Ivan's muted breathing suggested that all he wanted was a word, a nod, to make him tear the Toff apart.

Leah looked into the bag and then began to rummage inside.

The gun was there; everything was there, except the lipstick. What would she do when she knew that it was gone?

CHAPTER ELEVEN

The Silent Multitude

ALL HER POISE and all her calmness could not hide the tension in Leah Sharp. Rollison sensed it and admired her the more because of the way she kept feeling in the bag, although she must have known that the lipstick was not there.

At last, she turned and tossed it on to a chair beneath a small window. Its passing made the chintz curtains flutter.

'Where is it?' she asked softly.

'What's missing, Leah?' cried Micky Ogilvie.

'Be quiet, Red,' she said and stared into Rollison's eyes and repeated, 'Where is it?'

Ivan was very close. His hand was on Rollison's shoulder and, if he closed it, the grip would hurt. Rollison stood very still, watching Leah, meeting her challenge. Outside, the sun was so bright and a lark sang and from a part of the field there came a hammering; but those were things and sounds apart.

'Call him off, Leah,' said Rollison, gently.

Where is it?'

'Call him off.'

If she refused, then Ivan would try to make him talk and it seemed obvious now that, like a beast superbly trained, he would do whatever his mistress told him.

Leah said more softly, 'Where *is* it?'

'Leah,' said Rollison in a honey-sweet voice, 'I had a dream last night but didn't enjoy it. I dreamt that some friends of mine, big powerful chaps, were thrown about as if they were pieces of straw. Some of them got hurt. If they find the man who threw them about, they'll do all the harm they can. His size and his strength won't help him then. Just call him off.'

Would he win? Or was her feline strength too great for him?

He heard the harsh breathing of the giant behind him and, in some ways more alarming, could see the look of strain, almost fear, on Micky's face. Neither spoke; it was as if each realised that this duel was exclusively Leah's and Rollison's and that no one else must intrude.

The silence lengthened.

The sun still shone upon Leah.

She looked past Rollison to Ivan.

'Go back to the booth, Ivan,' she said. 'I'll send for you if I want you.'

Rollison felt as if he had stopped after running a long, long way. He wanted to sit down. He wanted to wipe his forehead. But he maintained a set grin and simply watched Leah. For the first time, he began to doubt whether her command of the giant was absolute; for Ivan's manner, the very sound of his breathing, suggested that he was going to revolt.

But she won, for Ivan turned away.

'Send Bimbo here, to run messages,' Leah called after him.

'Already I do that,' said Ivan. 'And this man—'

'I'll look after this man.'

'And she will, too.' That came from Micky. It was out of place, very badly timed; it made him seem silly. In fact, he looked silly; and insignificant. He lay back on his pillows, grinning, showing his fine white teeth. His creamy skin was marred in three places by scratches and now Rollison saw that his left hand was bandaged, too.

'Hallo,' said the Toff, as Leah opened the bottom half of the door and he stepped in. 'Been fighting?'

'I know who he is, now,' Leah said. 'He was here last night. If it hadn't been for him, you would have been in a bad way, Red.'

'Well, well, do I owe the man me life? Shouldn't I be full of loving gratitude for him, then?' asked Micky, trying to be bright and breezy and blasé; and falling far short. It was hard to say why. The words sounded hollow; as if he knew that his audience wasn't really interested. 'It wouldn't be the great Richard Rollison, now, would it? The great Toff, as they say? Why, then, where's the monocle and the top-hat? Don't tell me the picture they paint of you isn't the true one.'

Leah's quick eyes held a sharper interest.

'*Are* you the Toff?'

'A most ridiculous name,' murmured Rollison, apologetically. 'I'm always having to explain it away. But the romantics must have their moment of silly triumph, mustn't they? Thank you for sending Ivan the Terrible away.'

'I can easily bring him back.'

'Oh, no doubt, but I shan't let him get behind me again,' said Rollison. 'Once scared, twice spry.'

He liked the way laughter sprang to her eyes; and noticed that it didn't spring to Mick's. Sal's boyfriend was not feeling amused but was deadly serious. Perhaps he was afraid of what Rollison would think of Sal's boyfriend being so much at home with Leah. He did not know that the Toff had heard his quarrel with Leah.

Was that his chief worry?

'Where is the lipstick?' Leah broke the silence.

'As a matter of fact,' said the Toff, taking out his gold cigarette-case and proffering it to her, 'I've left it with a friend. At a bank. In a vault. Wrapped up and labelled: *Poison, not to be Taken.*'

She didn't answer as she took a cigarette; but she disliked what he said because he made it sound like the truth.

Micky didn't like it, either. He moved himself abruptly and said, 'Don't be so ruddy clever! Where is it?'

'So far, the police don't know that I found it or what was in it,' said Rollison. 'I always like to give the suspect the benefit of the doubt, especially if she happens to be more beautiful than Venus and Juno would be if they merged their many charms. May I sit down?' He flicked his lighter and, when Leah took a light, dropped into the easy-chair; he sat on the bag. 'Oh!' he exclaimed. 'Sorry!' He wriggled and brought it out. 'Yours, I believe.'

'Will you talk!' cried Micky.

Rollison looked upon him much as an eagle would look at a budgerigar. The glance said that he did not like Micky, that he had no time for him, that he wasn't interested in his looks, his thoughts, his heart or his mind; if he had a mind.

'I'd like to talk to you, Leah,' he said. 'But not here.'

'Don't you go anywhere with him!' Micky flared up. 'He'll cheat you, he's just a cheap stooge.'

'Unjust,' reproved the Toff. 'Where shall we go, Leah?'

Outside,' she said.

'Be careful,' Micky cried, 'he's a clever devil!'

She glanced at him and said, 'Don't shout so much, Red.' She picked the spoon out of the sink and looked at a basin, half-filled with what looked like cake-mix; and a cake-tin, also half-filled. 'I'll just put this in the oven,' she added.

It was a little oven, in one corner. Leah scraped out the bowl with a preoccupied but expert manner, opened the oven door and pushed the tin in. Then she washed her hands at a sink which Rollison hadn't noticed, dried them and took off a small plastic apron. She had a tiny waist and her stomach was as flat as a girl's of seventeen.

Micky the Red watched her tensely all the time.

'Leah,' he began, 'don't let Rollison fool you. He's a crawler.'

'As apart, I presume, from a lickspittle,' murmured Rollison. 'Don't make me dislike you more than I do, Micky. At the moment, I'm preparing a report for Sal and don't want to give her too many shocks.'

Micky looked as if he'd been kicked.

Rollison opened the door and Leah Sharp went out. The sun struck at her again and made her beauty blaze; and Rollison's heart beat much faster than its wont. For a woman to have that effect was phenomenal. She looked at him sideways out of her magnificent eyes and walked, erect and graceful, away from the caravan towards another, painted red. She carried herself as did women from the east, breast thrust forward, shoulders back, as if she were carrying a gleaming copper pitcher on her head.

Near the two caravans were half a dozen trees, an odd mixture of oak and beech and ash. Leah reached these and turned to face Rollison in the shade.

He knew that Ivan was watching from afar off. A little black-faced boy was quite near. Bimbo? The curtain at the window of Leah's caravan fluttered and Micky's creamy face and red hair appeared.

Rollison waited and they sized each other up, man and woman wary antagonists, each expecting a sudden stabbing sortie; yet with it all, a measure of respect.

'Where is the lipstick?' she asked, at last.

'I've told you. How did you get it?'

'That is my affair,' Leah said.

'The police might take a different view.'

Her lips curled slightly and the gleam in her eyes might have been of mockery.

'So Red was right,' she said.

'Red could be right.' Rollison didn't smile. 'Have you ever heard a boy or a girl screaming for cocaine? Have you ever seen them scratching and grovelling, begging and pleading, for the dope they've been used to but can't get any more? You've a good mind and a lovely body, Leah. Do you like the idea of smashing minds and bodies until they're broken, crippled things—no use to themselves or man or beast, to wife or lover?'

'What a flow of words you have,' she mocked.

'Do you like the idea, Leah?'

'How much will you take for the lipstick?' she asked, 'complete with its contents?'

He felt a surge of anger and an impulse to strike her because of the mockery in her eyes. He fought back the impulse but there was a change in his poise and she noticed it. She seemed to gather herself up, as if to resist assault, and glanced towards the little black boy. He stood, round-eyed and patient, with a smile on his thick red lips.

'Leah,' said the Toff softly, 'the dope isn't for sale and I'm not for sale, either. I could take it to the police and tell them where I found it and you'd be inside a police cell within the hour. How would you like that? You'd be imprisoned in four walls, one of them made of iron bars. And they wouldn't let you out.'

The colour faded from her cheeks and a shadow touched her eyes; a shadow of fear.

'I want to know how you got it, where it was going, who gave it to you,' said Rollison, 'and sooner or later I'll find out. The easy way would be for you to tell me. If you haven't my address—'

He slipped a visiting-card from his pocket. One side carried just his name and address; the other a pencilled sketch, carelessly done, of a monocle, a top-hat, a cigarette in a holder and a bow tie; a face without an outline which had become almost a coat of arms; or, if one preferred the phrase, a family crest.

'I'll be seeing you,' he said. 'Don't trust Micky, don't trust anyone and don't send Ivan the Terrible because even Ivan could get hurt. If you take my advice—'

He stopped.

She said swiftly, 'Well, what?'

'Hide Ivan,' he said. 'Sooner or later the police are going to catch on.'

He turned on his heel and walked away. The little black boy watched him, round-eyed. He sensed that woman's gaze, too, and wished that he had eyes at the back of his head, so as to see her expression. He did see Micky the Red's.

As he drew nearer the Big Top, the fighting booths and the stalls, Rollison watched Ivan. The giant, not far from the Rolls-Bentley, didn't move. Other men had appeared and stood about, idly; they were in untidy clothes, wearing caps and chokers, smoking, looking listless and disinterested but actually as sharp as needles. Rollison saw the man with the huge hands whom Micky had attacked.

There was no friendly face. Bill Ebbutt of the East End hadn't yet arrived and none of Bill's men was here.

Rollison climbed into the car.

It was nerve-wracking to be watched so intently; to wonder what was going on in the minds of these men; to wonder what part they played in the mystery of the fair.

Blackmail and drugs held sway somewhere here, two of the ugliest and most vicious of crimes. To save themselves from being found out, such men as these would kill — as Sal's maid had been killed.

Rollison started the engine; it was loud in the quiet.

They still stared at him, the men with menacing insolence, some of the women with grins of derision. Then they began to move in on him. Two went to the gate, which was open, and shut it.

Ivan the Terrible drew nearer.

Then a youth threw a stone.

CHAPTER TWELVE

The Gauntlet

THE STONE CLANGED against the pearl grey wing of the Rolls-Bentley and dropped to the grass. The Toff managed to keep his gaze off the spot where it had made an inevitable blemish in the smooth cellulose. The barricade across the gateway made it impossible to drive through; and all other ways out of the field were also barred.

Leah wasn't in sight; but the little black boy was—breathing hard; as if he had come running. It was easy to understand what had really happened. Leah had telephoned to the men and given orders for this silent, menacing approach.

A gold lipstick case, not Leah's but like it, was in his pocket.

A stone whizzed past his head.

Rollison stopped the car and sat for a moment, looking at Ivan the Terrible who was approaching from the right. Then Rollison climbed out and closed the door quietly. They stood on either side of the car. The giant's amber eyes burned with anger which it was easy to believe Leah had inspired.

'Tear him to little pieces, Ivan!' a youth called out.

'S'right,' yelled a girl. 'Let's see if he cracks!'

Gusts of laughter and raucous voices came from the ring of people so thick now that there was no easy way through. They had headed him off; and now they were going to have their fun, watching him beaten up. They expected Ivan to do all that was necessary.

The Toff remembered the way those Yard men had been smacked against the wall.

He hadn't a chance with Ivan the Terrible if he allowed the strong man to get too close. He did not show that he knew that. He smiled upon Ivan, returning beam for scowl, eyes merry, lips parted. He leaned against the car and called across:

'When do we start, little man?'

'*Give it to him, Ivan.*'

'*Tear 'im to bits!*'

The shouting and the tumult did not die. It got worse—and Jake Sharp, massive, dark, unshaven, appeared from a stall, leering, jeering.

'You won't get away twice, Mr ruddy Toff, the old man's not here to protect you. Hand over the lipstick.'

Rollison did not answer him but lit a cigarette. The flame burned steadily from the lighter. At least Jake and the others could see that they hadn't shaken his nerve. He didn't look towards the road for salvation would not come from there. The fairground was a long way from the village, there were no casual passers-by.

Then he saw Ivan, who was moving towards the front of the car, glance away from him. Ivan's expression changed. Rollison did not look away from Ivan but straightened up by the side of the car. His one hope was speed: swift, demoralising action, taking Ivan by surprise and fooling them all. Of course, there wasn't a chance; but he had to try. He could buy them off with the lipstick case but from that moment he wouldn't count at all among the hucksters or the workers at the fair. And he had to count.

Ivan had rounded the front of the car and was watching him, warily. A good sign.

No one called out, now—until Leah Sharp spoke. Rollison hadn't heard her come near but wasn't surprised.

'Stay where you are, Ivan,' she ordered.

The huge man stopped. He had taken off his coat and was the original hairy man again with those magnificent killer muscles glistening beneath his golden-brown skin.

'You keep out of this, Leah,' Jake growled.

She ignored him; and, in doing so, made it clear that she was more truly in command, that Jake hardly counted.

'Mr Rollison,' she said, 'you can stop all this and save yourself a lot of trouble.'

'Really,' said Rollison, very clearly, almost inanely. 'How?'

'Give me the lipstick and the contents,' Leah said. 'The boys know you're threatening me with it, I won't be able to hold them back.' She was calm-voiced but intense.

'You may never have heard of it but there's a law of the land,' said Rollison brightly. 'The police and the public don't like beatings-up. There would be a charge and an inquiry and a lot of big and little Sharps would spend a few nights in cells and the ring-leaders, male or female, would have a long time in gaol.'

Leah moved so that she could see him, close to Ivan. She looked magnificent.

'Don't be a daft fool,' she said. 'We could all swear that you started it.'

'And we would,' Jake sneered approval.

'All right, I started it,' conceded Rollison. 'The police might believe it, they'd ask why and I tell them. They would be very curious about the little gold case and the white powder, wouldn't they?'

'There'll only be your word that it was mine,' retorted Leah, quite calmly, 'and hearsay isn't evidence.'

Rollison puckered his lips in a soft whistle.

'You know,' he said, 'you shouldn't waste your talents here, you ought to be a policewoman.'

'Mr Rollison,' Leah said, softly, 'I can't hold Ivan and the others back much longer.'

She was right. He could sense her struggle, almost a despairing effort, but Ivan was angry, Jake was vicious, the men and the women were out for blood. They'd come at him soon and Leah was giving him his chance.

'Oh, well,' sighed Rollison, 'enough is enough and only a fool refuses to accept defeat. After all, the odds are about fifty to one, aren't they? Not including Ivan.' He slid his hand into his pocket and drew out the lipstick case. The sun glinted on the yellow metal.

'That it?'

'Give it to me.' Leah moved forward swiftly.

'Oh, my lovely, that won't do,' boomed the Toff and his eyes laughed at her. 'Come and get it!' He held it up.

Leah was only two yards away.

He drew his arm back and flung the lipstick high over the Big Top; it went like a golden dart. Every pair of eyes turned, everyone stared towards the shimmering thing, every mouth opened—including Ivan's.

Then Rollison moved.

He went straight at Ivan, hooked the giant's legs from under him, sent him crashing. Then he raced towards the barricaded gate and won fully twenty yards' start. His luck held and he didn't stumble. He reached the gate and vaulted it lightly, turning his head as he flew over. Three or four of the men sprang after him. He turned towards the nearest main road, racing along the smooth surface, thirty yards in the lead now. But tough, young men were following, fleet of foot. He turned a corner between high hedges.

The main road was in sight two hundred yards or more away but the soft footsteps of the running men were close behind him; they'd made up at least five yards. He put on a spurt. The effort began to hurt. His face grew strained. They would beat him to a jelly and then hatch up some story to save themselves from jail.

Ahead, he saw the sun glinting on distant cars as they went along the main road.

A car turned into this road and came towards him.

He could hardly believe it; here was his one hope, the thing he had prayed for. He heard a shout from behind, glanced round and saw that the fairground men had seen the new danger.

Rollison didn't slacken speed.

The approaching car was an old T-Model Ford, a car of the half forgotten past, with big spidery wheels and antiquated sky-blue body. Rollison slowed down, gasping but grinning with relief which was nearly delight for he knew the car and the driver and the four men crowded in beside and behind the driver. This was Bill Ebbutt and some of his men from the East End, arriving here because Jolly had asked them to come.

Bill Ebbutt, huge, red-faced and boasting a narrow-rimmed bowler, recognised Rollison who closed his right eye in a wink which none could have failed to see, an eloquent plea for silence, then flashed past at a sprightly pace, all fear gone.

His pursuers had stopped; so had the T-Ford. Ebbutt would know how to handle this without revealing that he knew the Toff.

The main road was very near...

Rollison was still breathing hard when he caught a bus into Kingston.

At Kingston he was quickly lost in the bustling market, rubbing shoulders with housewives eager to save the coppers at the stalls, finding the cries of the stall-holders and the hum of traffic a warm and friendly thing. He had cooled down and behaved quite normally. He found some telephone kiosks and the operator had no difficulty in giving him the number of Sharp's Fairground.

A man answered, gruffly.

'Miss Leah Sharp, please,' said the Toff and squinted out of the kiosk along the crowded main road.

'Who wants her?'

'My name,' said the Toff with great dignity, 'is the Honourable Richard Rollison of London, W1, at the Princess's service.

'*Who?*'

'Just say it's the Toff.'

'Gorblimey!' the man exclaimed, 'you got a nerve! The Princess! That's good, that is!' He laughed, heartily, almost deafeningly. Whatever else, he held no malice. Probably these people would not hold malice, they would have respect for him because he had defied them. Jake might hate, Jake was mean-minded but the others weren't.

He hoped.

Leah said, 'Hallo,' in a voice that was exciting in itself.

'Why, Princess,' said Rollison warmly, 'nice to hear you again. We didn't have much chance for a chat when we last met but I'm longing to tell you what I think about you. Also, that precious little thing of gold and incense, so to speak. I've the real one still. Come and get it. I think you have my address.'

'Listen, Rollison—'

'And come alone,' pleaded the Toff. 'That is, your own sweet self. *Au revoir.*'

He gave her a chance to answer but she didn't take it. He rang off, stepped out of the kiosk—and then stood still, his smile gone in a flash of time.

The coconut-shy man with the huge hands was just outside. Two or three of the men from the fairground were with him. They were in the main street and the sun shone brightly on them. Dozens of people were passing. The market was just round the corner. But these four men were very close to the Toff and they knew exactly what they wanted.

The Toff said,' Go home, you fools. If you start trouble here the police will come out to the field. They'll hold Ivan and they might hold Leah. The only chance you have is to play the game my way.'

The man with the huge hands said sneeringly, 'So that's our chance, is it? Why, when we've finished with you—'

'Did Leah send you? Or Jake?' demanded Rollison. 'Jake, for a fortune, Leah wouldn't be so crazy. Go back and tell him to tackle Micky the Red. And to listen to Leah.'

They glared.

He moved, suddenly, swiftly, in front of a stream of traffic, crossing the road where they couldn't follow. He slipped down a narrow side street and hurried on until he found a garage. He mourned his Rolls-Bentley and hoped that Ivan had not vent his spite on it.

He had to wait twenty minutes before a taxi was available to take him to London and had a sandwich and a tankard of beer at a nearby pub.

On the journey the traffic was thick in Kingston and, from Putney onwards, just a crawling procession. It was two o'clock when the Toff turned into Gresham Terrace. Even before the taxi slowed down, he was sitting up and taking notice for outside his house, looking as creamily immaculate as ever, stood his own Rolls-Bentley.

CHAPTER THIRTEEN

Lovely Leah

JOLLY OPENED THE door before Rollison reached it. Jolly had something on his mind and looked so puffed up with his own importance that he was too pompous to be true. He began to speak in a low-pitched voice remote from all reality.

'Sir Harry telephoned, sir, to say that he has been called to Northern Ireland on urgent business. He would be grateful for a full report on—ah—progress to date when he returns.'

'Ah,' said Rollison. 'Next, please.'

'Mr Grice telephoned, sir, and declared himself to wish to speak to you on a matter of extreme urgency. Lady Gloria also telephoned with the same message.' Jolly paused and convinced Rollison that he was now on the verge of delivering the message of real significance. 'And—ah—lady named Sharp, Miss Leah Sharp, has called, sir.' Jolly paused again, deflated himself; and pleaded. '*Are* you at home?'

'Never more so in my life,' said Rollison warmly. 'Get Grice first and Lady Gloria second and put them through.' He beamed at Jolly who eyed him suspiciously, as if wondering whether he had been drinking, and then opened the door of the living-room-cum-study and announced:

'Mr Rollison has returned, Madam.'

He stood aside.

Leah wore her fairground clothes except for a floppy, wide-brimmed hat which was pulled to one side of her head. It made a beautiful frame, and it framed a beautiful picture, but it wasn't the right frame. She stood by the window, turned towards him, half-smiling, perhaps a little out of her depth.

'Why, Leah,' enthused the Toff, 'I didn't expect you so soon.' He strode towards her, hands outstretched, and she was so surprised that she put out her hands and let him take them. He drew her close and kissed her warmly on the lips, hugged her tightly then stood back, holding her at arms' length, eyeing her up and down. 'And believe it or not,' he said delightedly, 'you haven't changed a bit!'

Bewilderment vanished and she laughed. She laughed deeply and well.

'All friends again,' said Rollison and offered cigarettes.

'That's much better. Care for a drink or is it too late or too early?'

'I won't have a drink, thank you.'

'Perhaps you're wise. You need a clear head when dealing with rogues and vagabonds. It's wonderful to see you. Apart from the lipstick, why have you come?'

Her eyes were very steady; lovely; clear.

'I want to help you to find out what is going on at the Fair,' she said.

'Oh!' Rollison's expression was almost comical.

'I mean it.'

'I really believe you do,' said Rollison. 'Yes. Why?'

'I don't like the police about, it's worrying me and my father. I want to put an end to it.'

'I see,' said Rollison but he was not sure that he did.

This could be simple truth or a specious, optimistic attempt to make him believe that she was as pure as a snowdrop. He wanted time to consider and so moved and rang a bell. He was not surprised that the door opened with remarkable promptness; Jolly's ear had been close to it.

'Jolly, tea, please.' He turned to Leah again. 'Indian?' he asked. 'Or China?'

'Indian,' she said, weakly.

'Indian tea, Jolly,' ordered the Toff and appeared to shoo Jolly to the door. 'Make those calls afterwards.' He waited until the door had nearly closed then called, 'No, perhaps you'd better make the first one when the kettle's on. The one to Scotland Yard.'

'Yes, sir,' said Jolly.

He closed the door.

Mention of Scotland Yard had brought a change to Leah's expression but it would not be true to say that she looked frightened. She simply stopped laughing and smiling. Rollison became gentle-voiced.

'Honestly, Leah, you ought to change your dressmaker and your milliner. You'd be the Woman of the Year if you were dressed by a genius.'

'Do you *ever* stop talking nonsense?'

'My friends say no,' confessed the Toff, sorrowfully, 'but my enemies don't always think it's nonsense.   What are we to be? Friends or enemies?'

'It depends on what you do,' said Leah, warily.

'About this?' He took the lipstick case out of a drawer in his desk and turned it round and round in his fingers. It caught the light. She didn't come forward to take it but eagerness glowed in her eyes. He handed it to her and her fingers closed round tightly. Bewilderment showed in her eyes. 'Yours, Leah,' he said, 'but the evidence remains. I've the snow, photographs of the container, of your fingerprints, everything that would be needed in a court of law.'

She just looked at him.

'But I wanted to talk to you before we go that far,' said Rollison, 'and preferred my own home ground. I don't know what Micky the Red or anyone else has told you about me but I'd like you to know some facts.' He moved towards the trophy wall and fingered the hangman's rope; he was in great earnest now. 'Everything on this wall belonged to a murderer and each of the murderers died by hanging or of violence. Sometimes two, once three, people died for the same crime. They were accessories. You know about the law enough to know that accessories to murder can be hanged, don't you?'

'Where is this all leading to?' she asked, in that husky, throaty voice.

'That's up to you. What game are you playing? Who killed Miss Hardy's maid? Was it Micky the Red? Are you hiding him from the police and getting an alibi ready for him? And where did you get the snow? Don't you realise that you can be put away for seven years for peddling the filthy stuff?'

She didn't speak.

She was something incredibly, hurtfully beautiful but this wasn't her background. She belonged to the open moors or the forest or to the cliffs high above the sea. She gave the impression that she was trapped and searching desperately for a way out.

'Well, do you or don't you?' asked Rollison roughly.

'I know what would happen,' she said at last.

'Leah, listen to me,' Rollison said quietly. 'Murder's been done, drugs are being peddled and also there's some blackmail. The drug leads all go to you. If you're responsible, I'll find out. If you were party to the killing I'll help make sure that a rope like this is put round your lovely neck.' He moved a few inches to touch the rope and let the noose run through his fingers, softly, smoothly. 'But if you're being fooled or if you're protecting Ogilvie—'

He shrugged. 'Which is it, Leah?' She didn't answer.

There was silence when the telephone bell rang. That made her jump. He looked into her eyes and saw that she realised that this was the call to Scotland Yard. She was nervous about the Yard all right. He leaned across and picked up the receiver and said:

'Is that Superintendent Grice?'

'You know damned well it is,' said Grice.

'Yes, hallo,' said Rollison, knowing that Grice would realise he was talking for effect because someone else was with him. 'How can I help?'

Grice said, 'Just between you and me, the best way would be for you to go and drown yourself. But as I don't suppose you will— where's Miss Hardy?'

'At my aunt's,' Rollison said.

'Oh, no, she isn't,' growled Grice. 'She's flown. Get her back and don't lose any time about it.'

Rollison said, very softly, 'All right, Bill. But before you go—'

He paused.

Grice said, 'Yes?'

Rollison looked into Leah Sharp's eyes. Her expression told him that she was scared of what he was going to say. She didn't plead, just stood quite still and waited, her lips set tightly, the lipstick slightly smeared where he had kissed her.

'Any closer to the drug angle?' Rollison asked Grice.

'Are you?' Grice's voice was sharp.

It wouldn't surprise me,' said Rollison, 'it wouldn't surprise me at all. I'll be seeing you.'

He rang off before Grice could speak again.

Leah stood still but with her tension gone; instead she just looked tired.

Then Jolly broke the spell, coming in with tea.

That gave Rollison a chance to think about Sal. He would cheerfully wring Sal's neck. Obviously she had left the Marigold Club of her own sweet, tempestuous will. That was almost certainly what Lady Gloria wanted to speak to him about. Sal was making her own painful bed of nettles.

Jolly poured out the first cup then left the room.

'Leah,' said Rollison, wrenching his mind off Sal, 'you're in a bad spot. I'd like to think it isn't your fault. But add up all the counts. Micky the Red starts trouble at the fair... The fair is used to collect blackmail... Ivan the Terrible nearly kills a brace of policemen... You keep dangerous drugs in your handbag... And Jake and the men at the fair seem ready to do murder for you.'

'You guess so much,' Leah said and leaned forward, holding her cup, little finger crooked just a shade too sharply. 'Why should it matter to you whether I get in trouble or not?'

'I've a soft spot for all beautiful women. Are you shielding Micky the Red?'

'Why don't you ask Micky himself?' asked Leah. She sipped her tea.

Watching her, Rollison felt as he had before; a quickening of his heart, real excitement because she was so near.

'The police won't give you a second chance,' he said abruptly.

He heard the front door bell ring and wondered if it were Lady Gloria. He heard Jolly open the front door; that sound was followed by a man's voice, gruff, unfamiliar. It might be Ebbutt or one of his men, to report from the fair, and Leah might recognise him. Rollison actually started to get up as Jolly opened the door. If he announced Ebbutt—

'A Mr Jonah Sharp would like to see you, sir,' he said.

Leah jumped up so quickly that she nearly upset her tea. Rollison was caught fast between great relief and swift, hopeful curiosity.

'Show Mr Sharp in, Jolly,' he said.

'Very good, sir.'

In daylight, Leah's father looked very old, a grizzled veteran whose skin was tough, coarse, brick-red; flesh bulged protestingly above his stiff white collar. His black tie was a relic of the Victorian age, of the pop-in type and looking as if it were as much a stranger to

Jonah Sharp as Jonah was to it. He wore a pepper-and-salt tweed suit, the trousers so narrow that they talked of a fashion fifty years past. He brought the tang of the earth with him, of the great outdoors.

Leah had that outdoor quality, too; that hint of restrained savagery, something that was almost primitive. Ivan the Terrible also had it.

There were people Rollison would fool, people whom he would enjoy fooling. Jonah Sharp wasn't one of them. Jonah took one look round the room, which to him was luxurious and soft and effete, and showed how much he felt at a loss. He had a big face, lean cheeks and a very square chin; the jawbones seemed to thrust the ears backwards. His lips were well shaped but cracked and almost colourless. His grey eyes were restless, perhaps because he was so ill-at-ease.

Rollison said, 'Come in, Mr Sharp.' He offered his hand, Sharp took it as if he were relieved at being welcomed. Certainly he looked more at ease as he shot a glance at Leah that wasn't all parental concern. 'What can I do for you?' went on Rollison. 'Would you care for a cup of tea?'

'No, I wouldn't,' said Jonah Sharp, bluntly, 'I didn't come for that, Mr Rollison, I came to apologise to you for the way my men carried on this afternoon.'

Leah flushed.

'They were a lot of damned fools,' said Jonah, in a gruff voice, 'and I've given them a piece of my mind, my son included.' The glare he shot at Leah suggested that he couldn't wait to give her another, more rugged piece.

'You're welcome to visit my fair and depart in peace any time, Mr Rollison. If you were hurt—'

'But I wasn't hurt at all,' said Rollison, hastily. 'That was more to your credit than to they damned fools,' Jonah said bluffly. He snapped his fingers several times, impatiently. 'There was something else, what was it, now? Ah, I remember!' His face brightened. 'If there's any damage to your moty-car, have it repaired and send me the bill.'

There was a pause. Then:

'I will,' said Rollison, quietly. 'Thank you, Mr Sharp.'

'And now, daughter,' said Jonah Sharp to Leah, 'we'll be going.' He didn't add, except with his expression:

'And I want a talk to *you*.'

CHAPTER FOURTEEN

Death At The Fair

ROLLISON DID NOTHING to try to stop them.

As he closed the front door behind them, he moved round to Jolly who appeared from the kitchen. Jolly seemed to be on his toes, anticipating the next move.

Get after them, Jolly, and try to keep 'em in sight. If they have a row, the sooner we hear about it the better. Tell Bill Ebbutt that, if you get a chance.'

'I will, sir. You haven't forgotten that Lady Gloria would like you to call her.'

'No,' said Rollison, 'I'll do that right away.'

But he didn't.

He stood at a favourite spot, by the window of the big room, with his back to the desk, the trophy wall and the rope. He could see into the street and, by craning his neck, see any car parked opposite his front door. Father and daughter appeared and got into a big old American car. The man took the wheel and the car moved off. Before it reached the corner, Jolly had appeared and hurried to the wheel of a small Morris which he had parked and ready for emergency—as he did on every big case.

Both cars disappeared.

Rollison turned towards the desk and touched the telephone but didn't lift it at once. He had no doubt about what was worrying Lady Gloria. He ought to think about Sal and her folly but it wasn't easy. The effect of Leah went deep; disturbing was hardly the word. She could wear the wrong-coloured hat and the wrong-coloured lipstick and could be dressed by a third-rate dressmaker—yet still the real woman came through, with her beauty of limb and of body, exciting and compelling. And she had a good mind, too.

She might be bad.

Probably she was bad.

She had restrained the people at the fair and even Jake. Yet her father obviously blamed her for the fracas. Now, she and the old man were probably going at it hammer and tongs in a mighty quarrel, a battle of giants. But neither had uttered a word in attack or defence in his presence; this was a private affair, to be kept in the family.

Forget Leah...

Think of Sal, who had run away.

Pretty Sal with the innocent eyes and the jitters and doped cigarettes. He could picture her now, looking so scared. He dropped into his chair, pulled the telephone nearer and dialled; and recalled when he had last dialled. Then he had spoken to Leah whose husky voice had been disturbing even over the wires.

A woman answered. 'The Marigold Club.'

'Lady Gloria Hurst, please—this is Richard Rollison.'

'Just a moment, Mr Rollison,' the woman said, 'but I don't think she's in.'

That surprised, even alarmed him. Then he rebuked himself. Why shouldn't his aunt go out? Why should he expect her to sit next to the telephone? He found himself smiling. Old Glory was good; in a way, her whole life was a kind of goodness, Sal didn't know how lucky she was.

'Are you there?' the woman asked and again disquiet crept over Rollison, because the voice seemed to have assumed a new note, of agitation.

'Yes?'

'Lady Gloria left an hour ago,' the woman said, 'she was going to see you.'

Rollison didn't speak.

To walk from the Marigold Club to Gresham Terrace wouldn't take more than twenty-five minutes, even for an old woman who didn't feel like hurrying. And when Lady Gloria walked, she seldom dawdled. Disquiet grew into fear.

'*Are* you there?' the woman asked, sharply.

'Yes. Yes, I'm sorry. If she comes back or telephones, call me at once, will you?'

'Yes, of course. Hasn't she been...' The voice trailed off. Then another came on the line; a different woman, speaking on an extension telephone.

'I'll take over, Lil—Hallo, Mr Rollison, Hilda Morant here.' This was the secretary of the club. 'I'm surprised that Lady Gloria hasn't arrived. She left just over an hour ago and I understood she was coming straight to you.'

'Delayed,' said Rollison, trying to force himself to speak lightly. 'Or waylaid by friends or shop windows.'

'Well, yes, obviously,' said Hilda Morant, 'but I'm surprised—she was very worried. Her niece left here just after lunch. She had a telephone call which agitated her and said that she must leave at once. Lady Gloria refused to let her. In fact,' continued the secretary, 'Lady Gloria was so determined not to let her go that Miss Hardy was locked in her room. It was on the third floor and she climbed out of the back window to the fire-escape.'

Rollison said softly, 'So Sal was as frightened as that.'

'She was certainly determined to get away,' said Hilda Morant. 'Lady Gloria decided to come and see you. If—when she arrives, telephone me, won't you? I know it's foolish but I feel so uneasy about it.'

'I know what you mean,' said Rollison. 'I'll call you.'

He rang off.

He went to the window and looked out, hoping to see his aunt's tall figure sweeping along the street. No one was there. He waited for several minutes and, although various people appeared, all were strangers. Old Glory had been worried, anxious and determined to see him; so she wouldn't allow anything trivial to delay her. She had left an hour and twenty minutes ago. Too long.

He telephoned Grice.

'I've been going to call you,' Grice greeted peremptorily. 'I'd have been through before but the Assistant Commissioner wanted me. What's this line you've got on the cocaine?'

'Tell you later,' said Rollison, 'and it's a slim one. Bill, listen. Lady Gloria started out to see me at three twenty-five. She hasn't arrived. She was upset because Sal Hardy ran away, climbing down the fire-escape.'

'She did what?' exclaimed Grice. 'Why, we're watching the place—here, hold on.'

He was gone for two minutes. When he spoke again he was angry, annoyed and puzzled.

'Miss Hardy must have climbed a wall and got away through

another building,' he said. 'My chap didn't know, the ruddy fool. He
saw Lady Gloria leave, though. You're worrying a bit early, aren't
you?'

'I could be. Ring the Division, find out if there have been any
accidents near the Marigold Club, will you?' Rollison said. 'She was
on her way here, remember.'

'I'll see what I can find out,' Grice promised.

He rang back, forty minutes later.
There had been no accident in the vicinity.
Lady Gloria was still missing.

From that moment it became a different case for the Toff. It wasn't a
question of helping pretty Cousin Sal or finding the truth about
Ogilvie or Leah Sharp. It wasn't a matter of blackmail and murder
and drug peddling. It was much simpler and sharper; find Old Glory.

He knew that Grice was busy, checking with men on duty in
Mayfair.

He himself called friends on the route, without any result.

Every minute that passed brought greater tension.

Lady Gloria had left the club in a hurry and walked towards
Gresham Terrace and on the way she had vanished. He found himself
thinking of fantastic things: like kidnapping in broad daylight. He
rejected them. She might have accepted a lift in the car of anyone
going her way.

Jolly telephoned, unaware of the disaster.

'Leah Sharp and her father drove straight to the fair, sir, and went
to a red-and-blue caravan at the north-west corner of the fields, near
a small copse. Sniffer Willis is near the caravan now and doing a
repair job on an axle. Shall I wait to report?'

'Do you know if Ogilvie is still there?'

'Mr Ebbutt says that he is, sir.'

'You come back, I'll go out there,' Rollison said. He knew that
Jolly must be wondering what had put the steel into his voice. 'Miss
Hardy ran away and Lady Gloria is missing.'

'Lady *Gloria*, sir!'

'I know exactly what you feel like,' Rollison said.

*

He drove as if his own life depended on getting to Gibben's field in record time. He slid past lorries and fast-moving cars and cut in ruthlessly, sent the lovely car roaring forward or swung the wheel so violently that it swerved as if out of control. Benevolent gods were protecting him for he had no accident and was not gonged by the police. He slowed down when he turned off the road towards the fair.

The road was thronged, as it had been the previous night, with children and youths and adults, all going one way. There was a steady stream of cars and cycles. As he drew nearer, he could hear the sound of the tinny, whining music, the hooting of the hand-organs. He could see the wheel turning and the cars swinging up and down the switchback. He left the car at the edge of a car park which was already crowded and almost ran into the fairground itself. Here, every stall was doing a roaring trade, every stall-holder was shouting.

'Roll up, my lucky lads... Three for a tanner... Try your luck... Best Sou' Sea Island Coconuts. Off wiv their heads and out pops a dusky maiden... Roll up, roll up!'

Children were screaming with delight or holding their breath in a kind of fear-filled ecstasy. Parents were harassed and anxious. Hands dipped swiftly in and out of pockets. Hoopla, the dancing ducks, the rifle range, the fighting booth; every booth and stall was doing a roaring trade and it was impossible to hurry through the crowd.

Rollison looked about as he elbowed and shouldered his way through. He recognised big Bill Ebbutt and two other of his East End friends and nodded towards the red-and-blue caravan. They followed and were not the only people to notice him. His height and his rakish good looks would have caught the admiring glances of most girls but both men and women saw him and were impressed by the glitter in his eyes which told of his driving fear.

Leah, Micky, Jake and old Jonah Sharp were here, the only people who might be able to help.

Bill Ebbutt edged a way towards him. When they met, Ebbutt didn't look at him but said out of the corner of his mouth:

'Fine old do up the carryvan, Mr Ar.'

'What was it?'

'Strike a perishin' light, never 'eard nuffink like it,' declared Ebbutt who was and looked an ex-prize fighter, possessing two of the reddest, plumpest cauliflower ears ever cultivated in the ring. 'Just before the crahd come, it was. That bit of stuff and 'er dad. Row? It was atomic,' declared Ebbutt earnestly, 'that's what it was, atomic. Then she comes out, looking as if she'd like to murder anyone who got in her way, and off she went.'

'Where to?'

'Don't ask me,' said Ebbutt. 'All I know is she slung 'er 'ook. The big cluck, Ivan Whatsit, come to see 'er soon afterwards but she'd flown. The redhead had gone wiv 'er.'

Rollison said abruptly, 'But Ogilvie can't walk.'

She 'elped 'im into a car, an' they drove away from the crahd,' said Ebbutt. 'I sent Charlie after 'em, wiv a bit o' luck 'e'll know where they went. Wot's up, Mr Ar? You couldn't look worse if they was going to 'ang you.'

Bill Ebbutt knew only Old Glory of Rollison's relatives and regarded her with awe, admiration and a curious kind of respect. He had some idea how the Toff regarded her.

'Lady Gloria's vanished,' Rollison said, brusquely. 'So has Miss Hardy.'

It did not occur to him that Ebbutt might not know a thing about Sal. He was thinking that Micky the Red Ogilvie had gone and Leah with him. They were more likely than anyone else to tell him what he wanted to know. He would make them talk; he would make anyone talk, from Ivan the Terrible downwards. But he needed to use his wits. Old Jonah Sharp would almost certainly want to help.

No one was near the Sharp family's caravans. Rollison went to the door of the old man's and tapped sharply on the horse-box door. He lit a cigarette and threw it away after three puffs.

It's a funny fing,' Ebbutt said. 'Sniffer would 'a told me if Jonah 'ad come aht. Where *is* Sniffer?'

No sound came.

Rollison tried to open the caravan door. It wasn't locked or bolted. He looked into the shadowy interior and saw only one thing.

Jonah Sharp sat in an easy-chair with his thick neck bulging over a cord instead of a white collar. His lips were parted, his eyes slightly open.

He looked dead.

CHAPTER FIFTEEN

Hideout

ROLLISON STOOD BY the old man's side, fingers on the thick wrist. Sharp was certainly dead; his flesh was already getting cold. He sat there with his ears closed to the bustling sound of the fair which had been his life. He had quarrelled bitterly, terribly, with his daughter and she had rushed away with Ogilvie.

Ebbutt was in the doorway.

'Mr Ar, 'ow long are you going to be?' His voice was a husky echo of its usual heartiness.

'Coming, Bill.' Rollison wanted time before anyone else knew about this.

He closed the door quietly. No one was coming and he hurried off with Ebbutt.

'What happened in there?' Ebbutt demanded hoarsely.

'The old boy was strangled.'

Ebbutt said, 'Damn it, Mr Ar, there's sunnink reelly nasty abaht this job.'

'Yes. Find Sniffer, check with the others, Bill. I'm going to Leah's caravan from the other side.'

'Going to tell the police?'

'Give me time,' said the Toff and gave what might almost have been called a smile.

The clamorous noises of the fair were nearer and louder but he was hardly aware of them. He was glad that there were so many people about; it made him less noticeable. He found his way towards Leah's caravan. A few stragglers were about, that was all; all the fairground folk were busy with their jobs.

Rollison went up the three wooden steps to the door of Leah's caravan and pushed the top half of the door. It opened. He stepped inside and shut the door. A good light came through the three small windows. He looked round quickly then began to search. Small dresser, tiny wardrobe, little dressing-table, were all built in; they yielded nothing. Suitcases yielded nothing, either. Every inch of space was utilised for storage.

Rollison moved everything, working with savage speed. He began
to sweat. He paused every now and then to listen to the sounds outside,
to make sure that no one was approaching.

He nearly finished the search without making any discovery.

Then he opened the door of a corner cupboard which served as a
larder, looked at the tins, remembered Leah's cake and opened a tin
marked: 'Flour.' He fingered the flour. He sniffed. He stood very
still while he raised his floury fingers to his lips and touched the white
powder with his tongue.

This wasn't all flour; it was mixed with "snow." There was a lot
of the foul stuff here.

The police would soon know about Jonah Sharp, would search
everywhere and within a short time would find this. Then the hunt
would be up, fierce, savage, for lovely Leah.

Would that help Old Glory?

He might be able to use his discovery as a weapon against Leah; to
make her talk.

He would bargain with a murderess, he would bargain with the
swine who trafficked in this beastly stuff, if it would save Old Glory's
life. But if he took this tin of polluted flour away he would be inviting
trouble and Grice would have to hand it out.

He put the tin back.

He left the caravan and was soon lost in the crowd near the busy,
noisy booths. He saw two helmeted policemen near Jonah Sharp's
caravan; so there was no need for him to waste time telling the police.
He walked quickly among the crowd and reached the narrow lane
leading to the Fighting Booth. A little man wearing a top-hat and
carrying a hunting-crop was bellowing:

'Come and see the strongest man on Earth—come and watch the
greatest fighting machine you've ever seen in your life! He's just
about to fight, now—Ivan the Terrible, that's the boy! Come and see
him make mincemeat of...'

Ebbutt appeared.

'Any luck, Bill?' Rollison asked abruptly.

'Yes,' said Ebbutt, 'an' nen agen, no. Sniffer was under the carryvan,
they'd coshed 'im. 'E's okay but never saw no one. Charlie lost the

couple in the crahd. They didn't go far in the car, Mr Ar. No one saw them leave, though, and the car's still arahnd.'

'Then they haven't left,' said Rollison.

Ebbutt managed a weak grin. 'Only *prima facie* evidence, you'd say usually.'

Rollison said, 'Feeling strong tonight?'

'No diff'rent from any other night.'

Rollison's expression and his voice were bleak.

'Care to tackle Ivan the Terrible?'

Ebbutt looked at the little man with the shiny top-hat and the hunting-crop and began to smile. This time, nothing could spoil his delight and there was nothing half-hearted about his smile.

'I'd eat 'im,' he declared.

'You wouldn't, Bill. He's good.'

'*And* want me dinner arter,' declared Ebbutt.

'Don't take any chances. But go in and, when Ivan's finished his present fight, challenge him again. Keep him busy for as long as you can.'

'Okay,' agreed Ebbutt and, because he knew the Toff well and had implicit faith in him, he did not ask the question which was burning into his mind.

'I'm going to look through his caravan,' explained Rollison. 'He's Leah's guardian angel.'

'Guardian *h*ape,' corrected Ebbutt. 'I'll keep 'im, Mr Ar, take your time.

Rollison moved off.

Dusk was falling and it would soon be dark. The sky was overcast, too, and a wind was blowing up. It carried the din of the fairground towards Rollison and the cluster of caravans and trailers on the northern end of the field. He knew Ivan's caravan; small and old-fashioned but motor-drawn. Most of the vans were in darkness, although in one a baby was crying. No one came to attend to it. He reached Ivan's and turned to look back at the fair itself.

Lights were being switched on, the generating plant was throbbing away, kerosene flares blazed at some of the booths; all this gave the scene a look of almost medieval savagery. But he was interested in people. A woman came hurrying and Rollison waited in the shadows by the side of the caravan. She passed without seeing him, a young woman with flowing black hair, barelegged, wearing a pair of down-at-heel shoes, a blouse which was off the shoulder because the buttons had come off. She ran to the caravan where the child was crying and opened and slammed a door; in a moment there was quiet.

Rollison walked up to Ivan's caravan. The wooden steps creaked. He paused at the top but heard no sound from inside. He tried the door handle and pushed; but the door didn't budge.

He took out his penknife and selected the skeleton key and began to twist and turn, gently. It didn't matter how hard he tried to avoid it, he made a scratching sound. The wind carrying those gay and gallivanting noises helped to drown these. A dozen tunes were being ground out at once yet the sound he heard most clearly was the sound of metal on metal.

Was anyone inside here?

If they were awake, could they fail to hear him?

He heard the lock click back and waited, pocketing the knife. He heard no sound from inside but anyone there might be fooling him; and a murderer might be there, someone desperate and at bay—and aware that a second killing could make his plight no worse.

Or Old Glory's plight.

He pushed the door open, gently. It squeaked. He stood listening, with his fingers on the handle, and heard the sound of breathing, very soft and steady; it was easy to think that he was imagining it.

He pushed the door wider open and stepped inside.

If Leah were here, would she *sleep*? Would Micky the Red sleep?

He could see a figure lying on the bed in the caravan but the light was too poor for him to see who it was. He stepped nearer.

Then he saw.

It was Sal.

Sal was asleep.

Rollison shook her vigorously and she did not stir, so probably it was a drugged sleep.

He was nearly over the surprise by then. He had expected to find Leah; Micky wouldn't have surprised him; but Sal...

He pulled back the sheet.

All she had on were a cream-coloured brassiere and panties and stockings which were rolled at the top, to keep up. He turned away from her and found her clothes on a chair. He managed to drag her dress on and fumbled with a zip-fastener.

The police might be searching already and they mustn't find Sal here. He had to get her away—and that meant the loss of valuable time in the main task of finding his aunt.

Leah might have helped him.

He carried Sal outside then took her to the side of the caravan and laid her on the grass. He pushed and eased her underneath where she wasn't likely to be seen. It was nearly dark.

He hurried back to the caravan and used a thin pencil torch to search inside, giving him all the light he needed. As he began, he felt the heavy assault of helplessness; what good would this do him? He might find out if Ivan kept a stock of the cocaine but saw little hope of finding anything to help find Leah.

He found nothing at all.

He would have to give up, get Sal away and try—where? Suddenly he remembered a receipt in Micky Ogilvie's flat for a month's hire of a caravan across the Thames from here. It was like rain on a hot day and gave him fresh hope. He turned towards the door.

A creaking sound, the kind his footsteps had made, came from the wooden steps.

CHAPTER SIXTEEN

Heart To Heart

ROLLISON MOVED TOWARDS the door but kept to one side. The creaking came again. He thought the door began to open. Whoever was coming moved stealthily. Had he seen the light through the window? Faint light crept in as the door opened wider.

A man appeared, just a shadowy shape. His right hand was thrust forward, he might be holding anything. He actually stepped inside the caravan and then stopped. Rollison could hear his breathing although he tried to stifle all sound. He stood there as if he were listening or looking for someone else.

Then he relaxed and moved more freely. He turned his body away from Rollison towards the light switch by the door. Rollison guessed what he was doing and narrowed his eyes against the light. As it came on, he said softly

'Keep quite still.'

Micky the Red stood there, hand still touching the switch. He spun round. He carried a gun in his other hand and fear or surprise shook him into raising it. He glared at Rollison who swayed to one side as the shot came. Flame glowed. The bullet smashed into the wooden wall and, before a second came, Rollison smashed a fist into Micky's jaw. Micky reeled backwards. The gun, the nearness of the escape, the dislike he already felt for Micky the Red, made the rest easy.

Soon Micky lay on the floor, unmoving.

Rollison stood by the partly-open door. Had anyone heard the shooting? Or the brief scuffle? There was the woman who had come hurrying to her baby; wouldn't she wonder what it was about and send for help?

There was no nearby sound.

Rollison picked Micky up by the shoulders and dragged him out of the caravan. It had happened so quickly, and was so quickly over, that it was hard to believe that there had been a brush with death.

Then he heard a whisper:

'That you, Mr Ar?'

'Yes. Who's that?'

'Charlie and me,' said a man who materialised as a dark shadow against other caravans. 'Bill told us to come and lend an 'and, didn't know which was old Ivan's box, that was the trouble. Anything we can do?'

'Take this chap to Bill's car,' said Rollison, 'and get him out of the fairground. Don't lose him. If you have to break his neck, don't lose him.'

'Where shall we take 'im?'

Rollison said slowly, 'Better make it Bill's gymnasium for a start.'

'Okay,' said Charlie. 'Anyfink else?'

'Not yet,' said Rollison.

They carried Micky the Red off.

Rollison went to the side of the caravan and picked Sal up. She hadn't stirred. A girl who had the craving for snow would do anything to get it. *Anything*. An ugly picture formed in his mind's eye but he did not let it stay.

He carried her through the dark night towards his car.

No one stopped or took particular notice of him.

It was only an hour or so since he had come here; and in that time he had found the murdered Jonah Sharp, a big hoard of cocaine and Sal, unconscious; and he had Micky Ogilvie a prisoner, too.

Yet it wasn't enough; not anything like enough. He had to find Old Glory. If Micky the Red were one of the crooks then she might be his prisoner; and Red Ogilvie had that caravan not far away, at Williton.

Rollison found the village on the other side of the Thames, half an hour's drive away from the fair. The fairground with its gaudy lights was visible across the river from River Way which was a small piece of land with a single caravan on it.

The door was locked. Rollison used his skeleton key, forced the lock and went in, hoping with desperate hope.

Old Glory wasn't there. He found no drugs and nothing to help, so he went back for Sal.

Jolly was waiting at the flat when he arrived and Jolly's expression did not falter when he saw Sal Hardy, limp in Rollison's arms, slim nylon-clad legs and tousled black hair showing at either end of a gay tartan car rug.

Jolly went to the spare room and turned down the bed, as Rollison brought Sal in and said brusquely:

'We'll have a doctor.'

'I'll telephone Dr Grayson at once, sir.'

'Yes,' said Rollison. 'Thanks. Grice's men are outside and recognised Miss Hardy, so I'd better tell Grice she's here.'

He looked down at Sal bleakly. He was on edge to get to Ebbutt's place and start to question Micky. Ought he to wait and hear what the doctor said about Sal? His mind was probing; restless; anxious; and Sal was almost a nuisance yet she needed help almost as much as Lady Gloria.

His next step *must* be the right one.

Tactics were all important and above everything, remember that it was above *everything*, he had to get Old Glory back. He could sacrifice anyone in the process; even Sal. Sal looked so pale and sweet and pretty as she lay there, with a sheet folded just beneath her chin, and one shoulder showing, creamy and white. Her dark hair was glossy and beautiful—and she was almost certainly full up with dope.

He swung round.

Jolly was in the doorway. 'The doctor is coming at once, sir.'

'Good,' said Rollison. 'Now I'm going to telephone Grice.'

'I'll come over and see you,' Grice said. 'Wait there.'

Grice was very much the policeman tonight and on his dignity; probably because he was being prodded from above. He looked very tall, angular and acid. The doctor had been and gone, Sal still lay "sleeping," and Jolly was in the hall—but Rollison knew that the door was ajar; Jolly did not mean to miss anything that Grice said.

'All right,' growled Grice, 'you told me that you'd found Miss Hardy because you knew damned well that if you didn't tell me something, I'd haul you in. Have you talked to her?'

'You don't listen well enough,' said Rollison, as tartly. 'She's been flat out since I found her. You can go and arrest Ivan the Terrible if you like but I'd wait and see where he leads.'

Grice growled, 'So you would.'

'That's right,' said Rollison. He wondered if Grice were really annoyed or whether he was simply trying to goad him into losing his temper and saying more than he intended. 'My doctor says that she's had a big dose of one of the cocaine drugs. I told you she'd smoked a few cigarettes loaded with the damned stuff.'

'Lady Gloria had a doctor to her before she ran away,' Grice said. 'I've seen him. Miss Hardy's in the early stages of cocaine addiction. You found her just in time.' That was almost grudging. 'What else do you know about tonight's affairs?'

'I found old Sharp.'

'What about Leah?'

'I don't know where she is.'

'She left the fairground with Ogilvie.'

'I haven't seen her.'

'Seen Ogilvie?'

The lie came easily. 'No.'

'Lady Gloria?'

'Don't be a complete imbecile,' Rollison said searingly. But he didn't like the look in Grice's eyes and was afraid that Grice had something up his sleeve.

It was brought into the open, briskly.

'Rolly,' said Grice, 'this has been a relation-ridden case for you from the start. I know what you feel about Lady Gloria but don't take chances because of her or anyone else. Keep your head.'

Rollison said, 'Yes, sir.'

'And let me tell you a few things,' Grice went on. 'Miss Hardy may be your distant cousin and a VIP's niece but she's a suspect for murder. She was at her flat around the time that her maid was murdered. I'm having her taken away from here under medical supervision. Understand?'

Rollison said slowly, 'Yes.'

'Another thing: Leah Sharp had a violent quarrel with her father tonight. Hundreds of people heard it. They've never had anything like that before. The old man threatened to turn her over to the police. No one said why but obviously he suspected her of some crime and didn't think she would stop it because he told her to. That makes her a likely suspect because he was killed with—'

Grice paused.

Rollison said, 'Don't keep me in suspense.'

'It isn't funny. He was strangled with a silken cord which Leah Sharp used for decorating cushions with—piping is the word. And the same kind of cord was used to strangle Miss Hardy's maid.'

Rollison didn't speak.

'And in case you feel like wasting time searching, lengths of similar cord were found at Miss Hardy's flat,' said Grice. 'Also, Miss Hardy's often been to the fair—at other sites, not just at Gibben's Field. She met Ogilvie when it was on Hounslow Heath. I think she made a lot of trouble for herself when she took Ogilvie away from Leah Sharp. I'd say that she was getting the snow cigarettes from someone at the fair and went too far with Ogilvie to please Leah.'

'Could be,' agreed Rollison, stonily. 'But why was the maid killed? And—'

'If I knew all the answers I wouldn't be here,' Grice said. 'And listen. Don't let the danger to Lady Gloria make you reckless. You know how bad this is now. Leah's in so deep that nothing will get her out—we knew that the moment we found the snow in her flour bin. Ivan's her slave and he could break your neck at one go.'

Rollison said softly, 'Yes, I know, Bill.'

'Don't forget it. Don't get any blood-is-thicker-than-the-law nonsense in your head. You won't help Lady Gloria by doing any kind of deal with Leah.'

'No deal,' Rollison said, still stonily, but he didn't mean that. Grice eyed him closely then shrugged, stood up and went out.

In the same frozen mood Rollison left, half an hour later, driving the Rolls-Bentley towards the East End of London. When he reached the corrugated-iron building which was known to all and sundry as Bill's Gym, he was beginning to feel more human; hope wouldn't die altogether. There must be a way of finding Leah, even if Micky the Red Ogilvie were no help.

First, Leah; then Old Glory. Grice and the police and the rest of the whole wide world could come later.

That was his mood when he entered the gymnasium.

CHAPTER SEVENTEEN

Micky The Red

IT WAS NEARLY midnight.

Two or three young hopefuls still smacked at each other in the two rings which Ebbutt's gymnasium boasted. One promising light-weight was skipping briskly because he could train only when his day's work as a barman was done. Two or three old fighters were sitting in a corner, chewing the fat. Interest perked up when Rollison appeared and he smiled about him, looking bright and cheerful because that was expected of him. He spent no time with anyone, however; not even with a man who was wearing a polo sweater with the insignia of the Toff—top-hat and monocle, cigarette and big bow tie—neatly embroidered on the chest in brightest red.

The Toff was known as a patron to many of Bill Ebbutt's "boys" for a vaulting-horse, some of the parallel bars and a punching ball were among the fittings supplied by him. This was, after its fashion, his home from home.

Ebbutt was in a small office, partitioned off from the main gymnasium; and there were two doors. One led to a cellar which ran beneath the Blue Dog, the hostelry which earned Bill's livelihood.

Bill was sitting on a stool, wearing steel-rimmed glasses and reading the *Sporting Life*. About his forehead and his sparsely covered cranium was a red ridge made by the narrow-brimmed bowler. A little grey hair was brushed with sedulous care into a quiff.

He squinted up.

'Why, watcher, Mr Ar. Been 'oping you'd come.' He put down the paper and stood up. 'Getting a bit restive, that young spark of yours is. Talk abaht blarney!' Bill sniffed. 'Says he wants to see you.'

'He's going to see me,' murmured Rollison.

Bill Ebbutt smiled as if in gleeful expectancy.

It was a clean cellar; whitewashed; perhaps a little dusty but that was really nothing to worry about.

Micky Ogilvie sat on a small, empty barrel which had once contained beer known, because of its excellence, as XXXX. The cellar was redolent of beer; but there were bins with gin, and whisky from the braes of Scotland, and even nice drops of port from the rocky hillsides of Portugal. Surrounded by this source of conviviality, Ogilvie looked as if he were a teetotaller thrust down here to suffer purgatory. He had one black eye. His right ear was puffy. His eyes were bloodshot.

His foot was no longer bandaged but his left hand was. He needed a haircut. In the fluorescent strip lighting of the cellar, his hair looked less ginger than brassy green.

Rollison looked at him coldly.

'I—I've been waiting for you,' he greeted but there was no insolence in his voice now; he looked badly frightened.

'Nice of you,' said the Toff sardonically. 'I notice that your foot is better.'

'It wasn't—never mind my foot!'

'But I'm interested in preserving every part of you,' said Rollison, softly. 'The police don't like hanging half a man.'

Ogilvie said thinly, 'Listen, Rollison, I'm not scared of the police for my own sake. I'm scared for Sal. Do you—do you know where she is?'

It sounded true; and yet this man was an old flame of Leah's, had made it up with her as if forgetting Sal.

'Let's have the truth,' Rollison said nastily.

'That's the truth. I—I've been trying to help Sal. I discovered she was smoking cigarettes loaded with cocaine and—well, I tried to find out who she got them from. I knew it was someone at the Fair.'

Rollison barked, 'Who?'

'I still don't know for certain,' Ogilvie said. 'I once thought it was Leah. I'—he moistened his lips—'I had an affair with Leah but Sal—'

'You were pretty friendly with Leah a few hours ago,' sneered Rollison.

'Yes, I know, I'm trying to explain. I thought Leah was supplying the reefers. I'd finished with her and I thought she was doing a woman-scorned act and trying to make Sal an addict. But when I went back there the night before last—'

'Why did you?'

Ogilvie said slowly, 'A man phoned me and said Sal's maid was dead—murdered. He told me if I wanted to help Sal I'd better go to the fair. So I went. When I got there, some of Jake's thugs set on me. Jake is Leah's brother. They all knew I'd turned Leah in, they hated my guts. I don't know who phoned but I think he wanted me to run into trouble at the fair. Leah's old man and Leah stopped it going too far. Leah took me in. We—' He moistened his lips again and even tried to smile. 'We had a heart-to-heart talk. After that I was sure Leah didn't know a thing about the cocaine.'

'What made you so sure?' Rollison demanded.

'Oh, hell—I just knew,' Ogilvie muttered. 'Leah isn't a liar and she—well, she had plenty to worry about herself. She'd been sent a lipstick, anonymously—the thing had a trick compartment and it was filled with cocaine. She believed she was being framed, in fact, she suspected *me*.'

Ogilvie stopped.

Rollison said, 'Quite a coincidence.'

'I'm telling you the truth!' Ogilvie flashed. 'To hell with you if you don't believe it!'

Rollison found himself smiling.

'Anyway, it's true,' Ogilvie growled. 'I've just been trying to help Sal and when I realised it wasn't Leah, I—well, I started to think. The only man I could hit on was Jake Sharp. I'd seen him in Ivan Waleski's caravan when Ivan was at the booth. Anyone who was trying to frame Leah would probably try to frame Ivan, too. That's why I went there—and walked into you.'

Ogilvie stopped again.

Everything seemed plausible; and his manner was convincing, his fears showed in his eyes.

'Micky,' Rollison said, 'why did you drop Leah for Sal?'

The younger man paused.

Bill Ebbutt, until then a silent audience, coughed noisily.

Ogilvie said huskily, 'It was her money, at first. And—well, Leah's a bit high-powered. Sal was—was rich. Then we started to go around and I fell in love with her. That's true, Rollison. I'd give my life to help her, now.'

'What do you think she's done?' Rollison demanded.

'I think someone is trying to frame her for her maid's murder.'
Ogilvie was very deliberate. 'I think the maid knew a thing or two and
had to be killed to keep her quiet. Sal's in real danger, Rollison. She
knows it. I think she knows why it was done, too—she's terrified.'

And that was true.

'If I could only find her—' Ogilvie began.

'Sal's all right for a while,' Rollison said and told Ogilvie where
she was. The radiance in the young man's eyes did more than
anything else to convince Rollison that his story was as true as his
love for Sal.

There was little else.

Ogilvie had rented the caravan so that he could spy on the fair from
River Way. The Sharps had some barges and also an old houseboat
in a backwater down-river; all this could be watched through field-
glasses.

He swore that he knew nothing of Lady Gloria's disappearance.

He had seen nothing suspicious at the backwater and told Rollison
exactly where this was.

By then, he was obviously all in and once he began to yawn he
couldn't stop. Rollison left him in Ebbutt's capable hands and went
out to his car.

The old houseboat was a new possibility and might be the only
one. It must have a visit soon but not yet; Rollison needed time to
think and desperately needed rest.

There was Old Glory.

There was a new understanding of Sal's fears, too.

And in spite of appearances, Ogilvie might have lied.

Rollison switched on his headlights as he turned into Gresham
Terrace; they would show up anyone lurking there. No one was. He
kept the headlights on until he stopped. He left the car with its side-
lights on and went to the house and up the steps. The cold and ugly
truth was that he was no nearer finding Old Glory than he had been.
Sal was safe but Sal didn't matter.

He expected Jolly to open the door.

Jolly didn't.

Rollison took out his keys. His man might be dozing but that wasn't like Jolly. Still, *anno domini* was an influence to be reckoned with. If Jolly weren't dozing, where was he? He wouldn't have gone out except on some urgent summons.

Rollison stood by the door, key in hand. It was after three o'clock. He was physically all in. The house was quiet but it was not silent. There were sounds, just on the other side of the door.

Jolly wouldn't stand there, inactive.

Who would?

Rollison said in a loud, clear voice, 'Oh, damn, I've left it in the car,' and turned and hurried down the stairs.

Who ever was in his flat must have heard that and must feel that there was time to relax. It was possible that the intruder knew about an entrance from the fire-escape, too, but it wasn't certain...

Rollison reached the street and made his way to the courtyard at the back of Gresham Terrace, then started up the fire-escape. It was of iron and gave off a little, echoing sound.

There was no light in the kitchen above these stairs.

CHAPTER EIGHTEEN

Back Way

ROLLISON STOOD ON the ironwork platform outside the kitchen door. There was a chance that Jolly had shot the bolts; if he had, it wouldn't be easy to get in. Rollison took out his keys and selected the small one which fitted the special lock on the kitchen door. He turned it, slowly and cautiously, but its final click came sharply.

He stood quite still.

There was no other sound.

He opened the door and stepped inside. There was rubber floor covering and he made no noise at all. The outer door had a double catch; and he fastened it on the first, then stepped towards the kitchen door. Outside here was a tiny hallway, leading to Jolly's bedroom and the bathroom. Rollison opened it cautiously. Light came through. The door leading into the hall was wide open and he could see a bright painting of a futuristic maiden, more points than curves, which had been presented to him by an enthusiastic and grateful "client;" like the dressing-gown.

Rollison crept forward.

Then he saw Ivan the Terrible, waiting, arms drooping, huge body clad in a monstrous, shapeless brown suit, staring at the door.

On the floor against the wall, tied hand and foot, was Jolly.

Rollison could hear the giant breathing.

Rollison had a mental flashback. He had never seen physical strength used with such brutality and casual ease as when this man had thrust the Yard officers aside. He could crush a man's skull with his great hands, could throttle life away, he could break bones as if they were kindling sticks.

Why had he come here?

Rollison had a gun in his pocket and could use it; but a shot would probably wake others in the flat below. A gun wasn't everything. The right grip on the back of the giant's neck, the right hold on his powerful arm; that was more like it.

Rollison took the gun out and held it in his left hand.

He stepped into the hall and was only five or six feet away from

Ivan. He looked neither right nor left, just watched the vulnerable spot. A snatch at that right wrist, now held downward and loosely forward, a quick wrench—and Ivan would be held in a hammer lock which he couldn't loosen without breaking his arm.

Could he?

Rollison was only three feet away, now.

Two feet.

'*Drop that gun*,' a man said thinly from the living-room door.

Rollison felt as if ice had been poured into his veins. He heard the voice, knew what had happened, felt the wild leap of his heart and saw Ivan turn—all in the same split second. The most frightening thing was the speed of Ivan's movement. The strong man's face appeared in front of his own, great mouth parted, big teeth showing like a tiger's; a scowling, snarling beast of a man stood in front of Rollison.

Then the man at the side threw something which knocked Rollison's gun out of his grasp. As it clattered, a sickening new world of fear was created for Ivan grabbed Rollison's shoulders. The great hands gripped with a paralysing torturing strength. Rollison felt himself lifted and then shaken violently, thrust to and fro, up and down. His teeth snapped and shattered, he lost complete control of all his nerve centres, his eyes opened and closed, his body seemed to be shaken loose and pushed around. The only sound he heard was in his ears—like the roaring of a waterfall.

Did death come like this?

Then he felt himself moving smoothly; and he came up against a chair. It hurt but that was all. He fell. He just lay there, a crumpled heap, quite helpless—and watched the enormous feet come nearer. Ivan's feet; they might almost be an elephant's feet, raised to crush him. An elephant's—'Don't keep talking to me about elephants!' someone had screamed.

Sal.

The feet grew nearer.

Another man said, 'Wait a minute, Ivan, he's still dizzy.'

There was something vaguely familiar about the voice but Rollison couldn't place it, didn't even think of placing it.

He heard strange sounds and knew that he was gasping for breath; it was as if he had suddenly become a victim of asthma at its suffocating worst. There were red spots in front of his eyes. He knew he was quite still; everything else was moving. The only thing he could see were the feet; elephant's feet. *Stop talking about elephants.* He heard movements and they seemed to hurt him; then a quieter sound came near and he felt something stinging cold on the back of his head. Next moment, it was all over his head.

Water; from a sponge.

He gasped and moved.

'Give him five minutes,' said the man with the sponge.

Rollison heard that as a blessed message of relief. Five minutes. He was almost beginning to think again, to recover from the shock.

Five minutes.

That voice.

That dripping sponge.

Rollison lifted his head and could see it and the hand which held it. He had never seen such a hand. It was enormous. If elephants had hands, that was the kind of hand that elephants would have. *Stop talking about elephants.* Of course, he had seen those hands before; they were the hands of the man in charge of the coconut shy at the fair.

Why be surprised?

'Pick him up,' said the man with the hands, 'and put him in that chair.'

The foot moved; Rollison shrunk away but it was like trying to move out of the way of an—*no*! He held his breath but unexpectedly he was lifted gently, carried smoothly into the living-room and placed in one of his own armchairs—the chair in which Leah had sat. It was near the trophy wall.

Ivan moved away.

'Like a drink?' asked the man with the big hands.

'Ed,' said Ivan, speaking for the first time in a voice so deep that it startled Rollison, 'you are too soft with the man.' It was almost "der man."

'Try this my way,' urged Ed. 'He's no mug, he knows when he's had enough. If he don't, you can always shake him up again. Couldn't he, Toff?'

Ed was pouring out brandy in a glass little larger than a thimble. Rollison took it. His hand wasn't steady but he spilled very little. When he put the glass on a small table by the side of the chair, it toppled to one side. Ed of the big hands gave a little giggling laugh. It was the first time that Rollison suspected he was nervous and suffering from nervous reaction. Another thing that became obvious was Ivan the Terrible's menacing stillness. He stood a few feet away from Rollison. His arms hung down like the arms of a gorilla and his face was quite set and expressionless. Yet Rollison knew that if he made a single false move, that human tornado would descend upon him again; and he dared not face it.

Then Ivan spoke.

'Vere,' he asked, 'iss Leah?'

The shaking had been terrifying. The whole incident had done more to weaken the Toff's faith in himself than any single incident in years. Yet he was still capable of being utterly astounded. '*Vere iss Leah?*' The question came as simply as that but it came from an elemental creature.

Rollison didn't speak.

Ivan bunched his hands. It was little more than a reflex action but it was menace in its own right.

'I spoke to you. *Vere iss Leah?*'

If Rollison said the obvious and the truthful thing, what would happen? He didn't need much telling. Ivan would move forward and swing his great arms and the tornado would come all over again. There were things which could not be borne; that was one of them. Suddenly, frighteningly, this became a battle of wits; and Rollison's sneaking hope lay in Ed's nervousness and Ivan's devotion to Leah.

Rollison muttered, 'Where do you think Leah is?'

Ivan was puzzled; so much a fool that he was almost too much a fool.

'We t'ink she iss here,' he said and glanced at the door.

'But she isn't,' said Ed. 'Where is she? Don't make any mistake, old Toff, you'll get another dose of Ivan's shake-the-mixture-as-before if you don't talk. Where is she?'

'I'll tell you one thing,' Rollison said. 'She's with Micky.'

Ed sneered, 'As if we didn't know.'

'Just vun more chance,' Ivan the Terrible said, in his almost inaudible growl. 'Vere iss Leah?'

'Before we go any farther,' Rollison made himself say, 'what's it worth to you if I tell—'

He saw disaster coming.

Ed couldn't stop it; Rollison couldn't stop it; a nine-foot wall would have had difficulty in stopping it. Ivan moved, hauled him out of the chair with one hand and buffeted him savagely across the face with the other. His head and shoulders seemed to part company; pain screamed.

He heard voices, far off.

He was dropped back into the chair and, when his head began to steady, he understood Ed to remonstrate with Ivan, saying:

'Okay, so he knows where she is. But if you kill him first, he can't tell you, can he? Be your age.'

The room was there, the men were still there and Ivan was only two yards away, eyes bloodshot and vicious-looking. On his own, he wouldn't have stopped. Until then, Rollison had just been a victim, feeling powerless without realising that he was at the end of his tether anyhow, that he had put in three men's work that day. Now, he felt sore. It was partly because he remembered Old Glory standing where the giant stood now, breathing a different kind of defiance. And it was partly because his jaw hurt, his head hurt and his shoulders ached.

Then he saw the hangman's rope, on its strong bracket.

It was only a foot or two away from him. It had dangled over Jolly's head and above Grice's head and now it could easily dangle over Ivan's.

It had to.

'Listen, *Mister* Toff, stop stalling,' Ed said. 'I may not be able to pull him off, next time. Where's Leah?'

'Dat's right,' coughed Ivan. 'Vere iss she?'

Rollison said heavily, wearily, 'All right, I know when I've had enough. Oh God, my head!' He closed his eyes and made groaning sounds which wouldn't win any sympathy but might help to fool Ivan and Ed. 'The top drawer, in that desk,' he said. 'This side.'

He pointed.

Ivan turned. The man's speed of movement was bewildering; he could turn on a threepenny piece. He snatched at the drawer but it was locked; and it defied his colossal strength for the seconds that mattered.

'Don't you try any tricks—where's the key?' snapped Ed.

'I'm doing all I can,' said Rollison. He stood up. He swayed but kept on his feet. He had to do better. He slid his hand into his hip pocket and Ed watched him very closely; Ed expected a gun and dropped his own hand to his pocket. But Rollison only took out keys. He handed them to Ivan and the man snatched them away.

'Vich vun?'

'The one with the round handle,' Rollison said and winced again, only partly in pretence; neuralgic pain shot through his forehead.

Ivan sorted out the keys, found the right one and pushed it into the lock. As he pulled at the door his head actually touched the noose; he would probably not have noticed a wire hawser at that stage, he was so desperately anxious to find out where Leah was.

Rollison did two things at once. In a split second while Ed was watching Ivan, Rollison smashed a blow at his chin. Ed toppled backwards—and Rollison freed one end of the rope so that the noose fell over Ivan's head. He pulled the rope savagely. It bit into Ivan's neck, choking him. Rollison lifted an upright chair and smashed it on to the back of Ivan's head; and the man grunted, his head fell forward.

Ed was getting up. He'd dropped his gun and was groping for it.

There were split seconds to play with.

Rollison snatched a dagger off the wall. It had once been plunged into a living heart. He stabbed the glittering point into the back of Ed's huge hand and pinned Ed to the floor. The man was too aghast, too stupefied even to cry out.

Ivan began to stir.

Rollison pulled sharply at the end of the rope which buried itself deeper into the hard muscles at the giant's neck.

The maid had been strangled.

Jonah Sharp had been strangled.

Ivan was being strangled; and the Toff felt all his hatred towards the brute well up inside him. He held on to the rope and felt that he must pull and pull and pull again until the man was dead.

CHAPTER NINETEEN

Giant Killer

ONE THING AT a time was enough; but here were two.

The Toff was pulling at the rope and burying it more deeply in Ivan's neck; and Ivan was making choky, groaning sounds and beginning to wave his great arms.

Ed was staring at the knife which had stabbed through his great ugly hand and was pinning it to the floor; he was open-mouthed with horror. To free himself he must grasp the handle of that knife and pluck it out. It was as if he knew that once he did that, blood would flow freely over the mahogany-coloured skin. And as if he knew that it would hurt.

Ivan made more of those groaning noises; more animal than human. They were quieter; as if his life were ebbing. His arms flapped, now, rather than waved. He was leaning against the desk, his great barrel-like body supported by the drawer he had been opening.

Then sanity came back to the Toff.

He slackened the pressure, moved deliberately and eased the noose so that the rope just encircled the big neck but did not choke Ivan. Then he stood back and watched the giant. For a few minutes, at least, there was nothing to fear from him.

He turned to Ed.

He knocked Ed out with the butt of the gun; then pulled the knife out of the big, ugly hand.

Then Rollison discovered that he was gulping for breath; that a drop of perspiration had fallen from his forehead into his eye, misting his vision; and other beads were trickling down the side of his face. He made himself take ten deep breaths, then staggered towards the cabinet where he kept his drinks. His hand wasn't steady as he poured out a whisky and tossed it down.

'*Aaah!*' he gasped.

It was bad to feel as he did.

He knew that he had been frightened; that this was not due only to the physical exertion or to reaction after excitement and effort. He had been frightened in case Ivan should take him in those great hands and break his bones. He had known fear before, but never so great. He began to feel better.

He wiped his eyes, forehead and neck again and the world seemed a different place. He breathed more evenly as he went across to Ivan who still leaned against the desk, semi-conscious, eyes glazed and partly open, mouth wide. The teeth at the back were all topped with glittering gold. He was a man mountain of flaccid flesh, now, but would soon recover his strength.

Rollison wheeled the big armchair behind the giant and then placed both hands on Ivan's shoulders and pushed him. It was like heaving at a wall; but gradually Ivan moved backwards and then he began to topple. He went slowly. Rollison was able to push a leg beneath the giant's knees, so that he crumpled up into the great armchair. Next Rollison took the noose from his neck, draped it round his waist with much effort, drew it tight and then tied the rope round the giant's arms and right round the chair. If Ivan moved he would have to take the chair with him.

When Rollison finished, he was smiling faintly.

He turned to Ed who was stirring.

'Hallo, Ed,' he said. 'Having a nice time?'

Fear played strange tricks with men. A few minutes earlier Ed had been full of braggadocio and on top of the world, a man who was scared of nothing. Now, he was terrified; he looked as if all the strength had drained out of him with the blood flowing from his wounded hand and he could think of and see nothing besides that.

Sweat gathered like raindrops on his forehead. His eyes wouldn't keep still, his lips were quivering. It was a case of sheer physical funk.

'All right, Ed,' he said, 'I'll give you a shot to put you to sleep.'

He opened another drawer in the desk and took out a hypodermic syringe and a phial of morphia. With practised skill he filled the syringe, then bared Ed's left brawny forearm and plunged the needle in.

'Ooo-*oh*!' choked Ed.

'Now all I have to do is press the plunger and in a few minutes you'll drop into a nice, long sleep,' murmured the Toff and smiled into Ed's little, berry-brown face and terrified eyes. 'Or I can take the needle out and then use you as a target again. Say in the other hand.'

'I want—a *doctor*!'

'Later,' said the Toff. He was half-silly with reaction. 'I can send for the police, too. Ed, don't you know where Leah is?'

Ed was trembling from head to foot.

'Of course I don't'!'

'She left the fair with Micky the Red, did she?'

'I told you she did! Listen, Rollison, don't—don't use that knife again. It—'

'I won't hurt,' said the Toff and pressed the plunger home.

Ed winced when he drew out the needle and dabbed the little puncture with cotton-wool. Then he pushed an ordinary chair up and encouraged Ed to sit down. Ed did so, fearfully.

'Don't move, Ed,' warned the Toff.

He hurried into the hall. Jolly hadn't moved but he was relaxed and smiling faintly.

'Meet Toff the giant killer,' said Rollison inanely. 'Quite a night out.' He cut cords, briskly. 'I hope he didn't hurt you much.'

'Not really, sir,' said Jolly, in a tone that said he lied.

It was four o'clock.

Ed sat tied to an upright chair, unconscious. His right hand wadded and bandaged and if that were his only worry he would be a happy man when he woke up. Ivan was no longer in a stupor; but he looked bewildered. He kept trying to move his arms and to ease his neck. The Toff, smoking, sat on the corner of his desk and studied Ivan and wondered what the giant would do if he were given another chance. It wasn't a pleasant thought; this man was the kind who would kill as a beast would kill.

Was he?

Jolly, moving at half-speed, bruised but bright, had made coffee and cut sandwiches. He brought them in on a silver tray, as fastidiously as if this had been afternoon tea for a duchess.

'Take some to Ivan,' said Rollison, after helping himself. 'Ivan, why did you think that I knew where to find Leah.'

The huge man licked his great lips.

'You—know.'

'I don't,' said the Toff, quite steadily. 'There's nothing I want to know more. Well, only one thing. Where's Lady Gloria Hurst?'

Ivan looked blank.

'The old lady Leah kidnapped,' said Rollison.

Ivan still looked blank.

'Ivan, listen,' urged Rollison, 'there's a lot of you to get hurt. And I'm prepared to hurt it. Leah kidnapped an old lady, this morning, and you know where the old lady is.'

'No, I do not,' said Ivan. He spoke as if every word hurt his throat. 'I know nothing. Where iss—Leah? You must not hurt Leah, she is—so good.' He made that sound like "zo goott."

'I can nearly believe that she's fooled you,' marvelled Rollison. He could almost believe that Ivan had really expected him to know where Leah was, too; almost. 'Why do you think I know where Leah is?'

'Who else—would know?'

Rollison had assumed that Leah knew where Lady Gloria was; apparently Ivan had assumed that Rollison knew where Leah was. It was the same kind of one-track thinking and it wasn't very original. Rollison looked into the giant's tawny eyes and had a strange thought. This giant was handsome; a brute but a magnificent brute. He was a fit mate, physically, for such a woman as Leah. It wasn't surprising that he would tear people apart to find Leah but—

Where *was* Leah?

'Did any particular thing make you think I knew where she was?' asked Rollison.

'It was—obvious, wasn't it?' Ivan sounded puzzled. 'It is you who hates her, you who work against her, you and that little vixen-girl and Red. Oh, what a big mistake she makes when she likes Red! Always, I warned her. He is bad, I told her, he will do only harm. And she *laughed* at me.' He sounded tearful, it was almost pathetic. It gave Rollison an uncomfortable feeling that there were great depths that he hadn't plumbed. 'If you do not know where Leah is, who does?' demanded Ivan with sudden wrath.

Well, who did?

The last time Leah had been seen she had been with Micky the Red in his little car. Then, she had vanished.

Had she?

If she were in hiding, would she be at the fair?

Was she in hiding?

Did Micky the Red know where she was?

If Leah had spirited Lady Gloria away, why didn't Ivan know?

Could Ivan be goaded into saying more?

Rollison said slowly, quietly, 'Ivan, you're in trouble. You've been working with Leah for a long time. You've blackmailed people, you've supplied drugs to people, among other things you've helped to give Miss Hardy drugs. When the police know that you and Leah have been doing things like that—'

'It is not true!' roared Ivan. His voice took on a bull-like power, as if he did not know what a sore throat were like. 'Leah, she would do no such things! It is a lie, one great lie! *How* you say? Leah makes people take *dopes*? Ach, you are just a big *fool*.' He spluttered at Rollison. 'Not Leah, she would not do that, but Red, now, Red—*he* would do that, he would do all the bad things. You know why he beat up Ed, yes?'

Rollison said, 'No, Ivan, tell me.'

'I tell you okay! He tries to muscle in on the fair, yes. He wants to give protected. Yes? No, protec*tion*. Ed, he will not pay. So, Micky the Red and his gang, they break up the stall. That is what happen. And you—you, you big *fool*, you help him.'

If Ivan knew more, the Toff did not know how to make him talk. He was no nearer finding Old Glory, and he felt as if he were out on his feet.

CHAPTER TWENTY

Waiting

THE TOFF WAS in the hall of his flat.

Jolly stood by the telephone there which stood on a small table. The door into the living-room-cum-study was closed and Ivan and Ed were still inside.

'I certainly agree with you, sir,' Jolly said, 'it will be a waste of time talking to Ogilvie again. He has told his story and will almost certainly adhere to it.' Even in these circumstances, Jolly could be naturally pedantic. 'Are you sure you would not prefer to believe this man—ah—Ivan, than to believe Ogilvie? Ogilvie pretended to have a badly injured foot but wasn't seriously injured. He could have left the fair and come to London, couldn't he? He had plenty of opportunity to telephone Miss Hardy and frighten her into escaping and going back to the fair. He could also have waylaid Lady Gloria, because she knew him.'

'Sure?'

'Yes, sir. She was gracious enough to tell me that she disliked the young man, although she had to admire his irrepressible good spirits. If Ogilvie met Lady Gloria and told her that he could take her to Miss Hardy, she might have gone off with him.'

'Not her,' said Rollison. 'Not knowing the funny business on foot.'

'Ogilvie can be very persuasive,' Jolly submitted firmly. 'And if I may say so, sir, he would have a way with *any* woman.'

Rollison found himself smiling through waves of fatigue.

'Sal—Leah—Old Glory.' He spoke as if to himself. 'Yes, I suppose it could be. Then?'

'If in fact he was working on both the blackmail and the drug distributing, sir,' said Jolly, with the smooth air of a scientist proving a point by unanswerable logic, 'he would naturally wish to throw all the onus on to some other person. He could be trying to frame Leah Sharp for the drug distributing and Miss Hardy for the murder. Imagine this possibility—that Miss Hardy's maid discovered he was a criminal plotting to cheat Miss Hardy. In turn he discovered that and murdered the maid—so he would then have to get clear of every possible danger. He might see two ways out—using both Miss Sharp and Miss Hardy to save himself. He is a very plausible man.' Jolly was gently reproving.

'Most,' agreed Rollison. 'Proceed.'

'It would not be impossible for Ogilvie to have the—ah—snow put in the lipstick and in the flour tin,' went on Jolly, 'evidence so easy to find if the police were searching that I cannot understand how it came to be there unless the police were meant to find it.'

'Yes,' Rollison agreed. 'All neatly worked out and all possible. I suppose. And we're back where we started from. And Lady Gloria's missing. If Ogilvie is as good as all this, he won't talk. His life would depend on keeping quiet.' Rollison brooded. 'But he's the only line left.' He took out cigarettes. 'Call Ebbutt.'

'Should we disturb them at this hour?' asked Jolly. 'If you propose to arrange for Mr Ebbutt to give Ogilvie an opportunity to escape, so that he can be followed, you will want to take part in the chase yourself. And you are very tired, sir.'

'Meaning, I look half-witted,' Rollison said wryly. 'I also feel half-dead. All right, we'll take some rest. What would you do with Ivan and Ed if you were me?'

'I should leave them where they are, sir,' said Jolly. 'I have made sure they are quite secure. I will fix an alarm at the door of the room, so that if they should manage to get it open, we shall be warned. But I hope that you will be advised by me, sir, and go to bed at once.'

'Don't you need sleep?'

'I haven't exerted myself giant killing,' murmured Jolly, straight-faced.

He won a smile.

It was ten o'clock when Rollison woke. This time there was no Jolly by his side with tea; the telephone bell was ringing and no movement about the flat suggested that Jolly was hurrying to answer it. The Toff's head felt like a waterlogged sponge. When he pushed back the bedclothes, he discovered that his arms and shoulders were stiff; painfully, too. He remembered Ivan's grip; he remembered every-thing. He struggled up in bed and lifted the telephone by his side.

'Hallo?'

'Is that you, Rolly?' It sounded like an alarmed Grice. Rollison's heart began to hammer through a yawn. Was there news? Had the police found Lady Gloria? He couldn't make himself ask and took refuge in flippancy. 'I—yes, Bill. Yes. Must you disturb honest citizens in the early hours of the morning?'

'*Early!*' breathed Grice. 'You—' He paused and when he spoke again he sounded free from alarm. 'I suppose you were up half the night.'

'Three-quarters.'

What did Grice *want*?

'Who with?'

'Ivan the Terrible,' said Rollison, in a burst of confidence, 'but if I were you I would see what he does when I let him go. He paid me an unofficial visit and I hanged him temporarily.' He couldn't wait any longer and steeled himself to sound casual. 'Any news your end?'

'It depends what you call news. I can tell you that Miss Hardy says she had a telephone call from the blackmailer yesterday. She knew the maid was dead and ran away from the flat. Someone found out—a man with a voice like the one who'd scared her about the dope, she says. That is why she ran away from the Marigold Club. She went to the fairground, on instructions, then to Ivan Waleski's caravan. She says that she smoked a cigarette there and doesn't remember anything else after that.'

Rollison didn't speak.

'Still there?' demanded Grice, sharply.

'Oh, yes,' said Rollison. ' I'm still here. Is that all she told you?'

'Yes.'

'Did she implicate Ogilvie?'

'No.'

'Leah Sharp?'

'I've told you all I know about Miss Hardy,' Grice said. 'You ought to think yourself lucky. She says she didn't see Lady Gloria, swears she doesn't know a thing more. What are you going to do?'

Rollison said heavily, 'Get busy. Ivan Waleski's at the flat. I'm going to let him go some time during the morning. Will you have him followed?'

'Yes.' Grice was brisk.

'Better send two men,' advised Rollison, 'there's also a man named Ed. He—'

'Man with the big hands?'

'Yes.'

'That's Ed Garney,' said Grice, 'one of Jonah Sharp's sons-in-law. There is something else, too. Ebbutt had a man watching Jonah—a Sniffer Willis. Remember, he was hurt. He heard Leah and her father having their stand-up quarrel. He didn't see anyone else go to the caravan. All he remembers is lying underneath it, listening and pretending to be busy on the axle—and then being dragged out by the feet and banged over the head. He didn't see his assailant.'

'Pity,' said Rollison. 'Bill.'

'Yes?'

'Ivan Waleski *alias* the Terrible doesn't agree that Leah Sharp is a wicked woman. He doesn't think she would have anything to do with selling drugs and—'

Grice snorted.

'Be yourself,' he said. 'Ivan worships her. He'd lie himself to the gallows to save her.'

'I wonder if he would,' said Rollison. 'Okay, Bill. Thanks a lot.' He rang off.

Lady Gloria hadn't been so much as mentioned.

Rollison got out of bed and discovered that his legs were as painfully stiff as his arms. Already the day seemed ominous; dark and menacing. It held a kind of lurking fear which had come with the first ringing of the telephone bell.

He went into Jolly's room.

Jolly was fast asleep, looking old as he lay there with his thin grey hair unruly and his lined face slack. Rollison watched for a moment and then left him and went into the big room.

Ivan the Terrible, *alias* Waleski, was also sleeping. His head lolled on one side, his lips were parted, he snored faintly; an absurdly gentle snore for a giant. Jonah Sharp's son-in-law, Ed Garney, was awake; he hadn't recovered his nerve and jumped wildly when Rollison opened the door and called:

'Hungry, Ed?'

'I—I'm *thirsty*,' Ed muttered. 'Gimme a drink, will you?'

*

Two hours later, everything was laid on. Ivan and Ed were to have a chance to escape from the flat and the police were to follow them.

Unknown to the police, Micky the Red was also to have a chance to escape—but not until Rollison was there to follow him.

Over all this was a shadow—fears for Old Glory and her uprightness and sternness and her golden heart. In spite of Grice's warning, Rollison knew that he would make any deal to save her; would sacrifice anyone, not least himself.

A little after two that afternoon, Rollison left Gresham Terrace in the Rolls-Bentley. He did not drive straight to Ebbutt's gymnasium but to a friend's home. The big car was parked in a garage there while Rollison drove off in a battered but powerful Humber.

He left this near the gymnasium, went in and put on borrowed clothes. In these, he looked as if the East End were his home and his natural hunting ground. Cloth cap pulled well over his eyes, choker up to his neck, one hand in his pocket, shoulders hunched, his walk sluggish and ungainly, he looked no more like the Honourable Richard Rollison than Ivan Waleski looked like Leah Sharp.

At a little before three, Micky the Red Ogilvie "found" a way out of the cellar. It was a manhole cover which moved easily. He pushed it up. He saw no one in the backyard of the Blue Dog. He hauled himself into the Yard and tiptoed across it. One side was walled by the corrugated iron of the gymnasium and he could hear someone punching at a medicine ball, someone else skipping, Bill Ebbutt giving orders to a hopeful prize-fighter.

Micky opened a wooden door which led into the street. The only person in sight was a man who leaned against the gymnasium door, hand in pocket, smoking. Micky didn't give him a second look.

But the Toff followed; and was so practised in this furtive art that Micky the Red did not guess that anyone was on his tail.

CHAPTER TWENTY-ONE

Leah And Micky

AN HOUR AND a half later, Rollison saw Ogilvie go into the motor caravan which stood on River Way, that stretch of the bank of the River Thames not far from the fair. Across the water, which rippled in the bright sun, were the green banks of a meadow with a few cows grazing. Just in sight was a wide backwater with two barges, one almost submerged, obviously rotting away. Near this was a jetty with a houseboat moored alongside.

A smaller jetty stood out into the river from Micky the Red's caravan site. A little outboard motor boat was moored to this.

Before going in, Ogilvie went to the river and looked up and down; then peered about the trees which hid the caravan from the nearest road. Satisfied, he went in, unlocking the door.

Rollison saw him from behind a tree.

Two of Ebbutt's "boys," farther away, drew nearer to Rollison. He told them by sign language to get near to the caravan then he approached it himself. He heard voices and he felt suffocated.

Could Old Glory...?

There were small windows on either side of the caravan but the curtains were drawn. Rollison stepped from the cover of the nearer trees then reached the door which was in the side of the caravan away from the river.

He hadn't in fact heard voices; just a voice: Micky's.

'Yes, I know how to get myself out of trouble,' Micky said, 'and I know how to make you talk.' *Who?* 'Why do you think I smuggled you out of the fairground? Didn't I lay on a couple of friends to get you outside, risking becoming an accessory after the crime? I want to know who's working with you on this. Get that, Leah?'

So it was Leah and Ogilvie had known where she was all the time. His "couple of friends" must have brought her here after Rollison had come to look.

'I'll take that gag away but don't shout and don't try to bite me.'

Something of the old gaiety was back into Micky's voice when he went on, 'Or you'll wish you hadn't.'

There was a moment of silence.

'It hasn't improved you,' Micky said, 'but you'll soon be all right. I'll get you a drink.'

Rollison pressed close to the door.

Something splashed.

'That feel better?' Micky asked, after another pause. 'Just make up your mind to tell me who you're working with. Soon. Because I'm going to find out, I'm going to smash every one of you. If you hadn't tried to frame Sal—'

He broke off, as if words and emotions choked him.

Leah made an answer; Rollison didn't catch it.

'Don't try to fool me that way,' Micky growled. 'You're in this so deep nothing will get you out. What do you think I've been doing? Was your father in it? Wouldn't he go on? Is that why you killed him?'

Rollison heard Leah's voice; a husky whisper of sound.

'I didn't kill him.'

'Listen, Leah, we're alone,' said Micky. His voice changed, was suddenly pleading. 'You don't have to lie to me. You know that anything you say won't be evidence. Hearsay isn't evidence. So long as Sal's okay, you won't get hurt. So let's have the truth. Were you in this with your old man?'

'No—one,' Leah said.

Come on, talk!' Micky's voice rose again, he was beside himself with rage and fear for Sal. 'One of your brothers?' Apparently there was no answer and he growled, 'Leah, you'll get hurt if you don't come across. I'm not here to look at your pretty face, I want to know who killed the maid, who framed Sal.'

'But I don't know!' cried Leah.

There was a pause; a sound which might have been a sharp gasp; then a cry that was almost a scream of pain.

'I don't *want* to hurt,' Micky said, shrill, 'but I will. Sal's maid was killed, wasn't she? Your father was strangled. You've sent dozens of people, hundreds of people, to a little hell of drugs. I'm not sorry for you. I'm just sick of the sight of you. I'll break your fingers one by one if you don't tell me *who* is working with you.'

'No one!' cried Leah. 'Red! Don't do—'
Rollison pushed open the door.
'Hallo,' he greeted, amiably.

Leah Sharp was tied to an upright chair. Micky the Red Ogilvie was standing in front of her, his body twisted round, eyes rounded, right hand at his pocket. But Rollison had a gun in his hand. He closed the door with his foot and went slowly forward—then he realised that neither of them recognised him.

He pushed his cap back and grinned.
'Remember me?' he inquired.

Ogilvie breathed, 'Rollison!' He let his hand fall from his pocket. Rollison went forward and slid the gun out of Ogilvie's. Leah looked deathly white, except that the corners of her mouth were red and inflamed from a gag.

'Listen, Rollison,' gasped Ogilvie. 'I only lied to you because I thought Leah would talk to me and not to you. Make her tell us who she works with, who killed Sal's maid. Go on—make her!'

Only his laboured breathing broke the quiet. Then:
'Can't you *make* him understand that I don't know?' Leah said in a hoarse voice.

'She knows, of course she knows!' cried Ogilvie.
'Why did you kill your father?' Rollison asked her.

'I didn't kill him, Mr Rollison,' said Leah very quietly. 'I know now that the fair has been used for distributing drugs and my father thought that I was involved. I couldn't convince him that he was wrong.'

'He wasn't wrong,' Micky interrupted. 'He knew, you bitch!'
He struck at her.

Rollison caught his arm, felt a wave of furious anger and struck Ogilvie beneath the chin. It was simply because he had tried to hit Leah. Ogilvie backed away. Rollison moved after him swiftly, grabbed his arm and frog-marched him towards a narrow door and into a kitchen compartment. He closed the door and came back to Leah.

Ogilvie didn't come out.
Rollison studied Leah, aware of the intensity of her gaze.

Her cheeks and lips were very red and puffy where the gag had been. Her eyes were heavy with tiredness and filled with tiny blood-shot veins. Her clothes were creased and rumpled where she had been lying. But she was magnificent. He felt his pulse stirring and beating faster. There was no reason in the world why she should affect him like that but she did. Could she even dull his wits and senses by the power of her physical beauty?

Or was she telling the truth?

He got her another drink and untied her. Then he questioned her and she swore that she knew nothing to help.

Her voice grew firmer. He tried to make her contradict herself but failed.

He stopped at last.

A sound from outside broke the silence, sharply, touching it with alarm. Rollison moved round, dropping his hand to his right-side pocket. Two of Ebbutt's men should be there, yet he did not think they'd made that sound.

He whispered to Leah, 'Keep behind the door. I'll take the window.'

'All right,' she whispered.

She pressed close against the wall by the door and Rollison approached the window. He was near it when the glass crashed in. He saw a curtain billow, saw the broken glass flying. A piece cut his cheek but that wasn't all, that hardly mattered. Tear gas bit at his eyes and his nose, he couldn't stop himself from breathing it in. He staggered away, his senses reeling, struck the far wall and leaned heavily against it.

He heard shouting.

He fell, heavily—and then he heard other sounds, loud thudding, another shout; and a foot came close to his head, then something smashed on to the back of his head and he lost consciousness, as if someone had turned off the light.

CHAPTER TWENTY-TWO

The River

ROLLISON HEARD GENTLE sounds, as of water rippling against the side of a boat or against a high bank. He lay listening. It was a pleasant sound, welcome, restful, peaceful; and yet he knew that he was not at peace. He turned his head and pain shot through it; and memory returned.

He kept quite still.

They were the only sounds: water, lapping. Yet he felt quite steady, there was no gentle swaying as he would expect on board a ship. So where was he?

It was pitch dark.

His eyes and his nose and mouth smarted but not badly. He knew that Leah must have suffered from the gas, too. He wasn't sure about Ogilvie. He wondered what had happened to Ebbutt's men who were supposed to have been on guard among the trees.

He stood up, slowly.

His hands were free, so were his legs. He could not understand that. He moved cautiously then banged against something which moved and clanged—and brought another sound; a gasp.

'Who's there?' he asked, in a whisper.

The answer came hesitantly, 'Leah—Sharp. Is that—Mr Rollison?'

"*Mr*" Rollison!

He found himself suddenly choked with a desire to laugh; and then with a sense of urgency, of fear. He did not move again but said:

'Yes. Call out, will you?'

'Why?'

'I want to make sure where you are.'

'I'm—here.'

'Is Micky with you?'

'I don't know. I—I can't see.'

'It is a bit dark, isn't it?' conceded Rollison.

He caught his breath and began to move towards Leah. She wasn't far away. It was very dark; it was the kind of darkness that, he imagined, a blind man would live with. It made him stumble again and Leah called:

'Be careful!'

She was much nearer. She was keeping her nerve but he sensed her fears.

'Coming,' he said. He knew she was only a yard or two away from him. 'I suppose it's too much to ask if you happen to know where we are.'

He crept forward, shuffling his feet.

'I know,' she said and added bitterly, 'but that won't help.'

'It might. Where are we?'

'We're in the shell of a derelict houseboat,' she said. 'It's been broken up, there's only the deck and superstructure above us. We're tied up in a backwater of the Thames.'

'You mean, near the fair.'

Yes. Near Williton. Red's caravan is opposite—across the river.'

He remembered...

Leah was only a foot or so away from him. Although she spoke very softly, her words were clear and very distinct. He moved round and stretched out one arm. He touched her and felt her start. Still with a hand at her arm, he drew nearer, until they were side by side and standing with their backs to the wall.

'Relax,' he said. 'How do you know?'

'I heard one of my brothers say that this is where we'd better go. The boat—is holed. It's listing already.'

'Brother Jake?'

'Yes,' Leah said. 'Yes.'

Rollison had a swift mental picture of the burly, surly Jake who had always been hostile.

In the silence, the lapping of the water sounded very clear and close. He could feel no water beneath his feet; but Leah had spoken with a note of absolute certainty. 'The boat is—holed.' So water was coming in somewhere and would soon reach them; and then, as the boat foundered, they would drown. She felt a sense of inevitability and he could sense it.

'It's listing,' she repeated. 'They—holed it.'

'They?'

Leah said slowly, hurtfully, 'Jake was one of them. I didn't recognise the others.'

Old Jonah had suspected Leah. Perhaps he had known only that it was one of the family.

Just Jake?

It was very dark and cold. The only warmth was where Rollison's arm touched Leah. She did not move. He found himself drawing closer to her and he slid his arm round her waist. He felt strangely calm.

She said, 'It's a funny way to die.'

'We aren't dead yet.'

'That's what Micky once told me about you,' said Leah.

Rollison found himself rooting in his pockets for a lighter; but it had been taken.

'Leah,' he said, as the cold crept into him.

'Yes?'

'Do you know where my aunt is? Lady Gloria Hurst?'

'No,' Leah said, quite steadily. 'I've told you the truth. I've been afraid that drugs were being handled at the fair and in the last few days it's become obvious. But I don't know who did any of these things. Once I thought—' She broke off.

'Micky the Red?'

'Yes, and no. I feared my father might be involved.' Her words were flat, pedantic. 'I didn't know until he came to see me at your flat that he wasn't responsible. He'd found out what was happening. The police had told him. He was so—bitter. You're the kind who don't need telling that a man's voice and education have nothing to do with the way he lives, his—oh, what's the word?'

Rollison said simply, 'Goodness.'

'Goodness,' she echoed and gave a queer little laugh. 'Isn't it funny, to be standing here with you and talking like this? I wish we had some light.'

'It'll come. So you know nothing about Lady Gloria.'

'No. No,' said Leah and leaned more heavily against him. '*Did* you find—cocaine—in my dresser?'

'Yes. So did the police.'

'I've never got along with Jake,' Leah said. 'I don't like his wife.

But I wouldn't have thought that he—' She broke off. 'I suppose it doesn't matter now.'

'It matters a lot,' Rollison said.

She didn't answer.

It was getting colder and if anything it seemed to be growing darker. Could it be? Was the darkness outside? Or was he blind? His eyes felt sore, as they would after a day of too much driving; or if grit had blown into them. Supposing he were blind, would it matter?

He thought, 'What's got into me? What's happening to me?' He moved away from Leah, so suddenly that he knew she was startled; he heard her catch her breath.

'We've had enough rest,' Rollison said gruffly. 'I'm going to see what I can find. Stay there. I'm going to walk round. When I get back to you I'll know I've made a full circuit.'

The fact that he had wasted so much time burned at him; time might be precious. He started off quickly and by the wall. Soon he went more slowly. His fingers ran along the wall; here and there joists got in the way and he scraped a finger on a nail. But the wall seemed to be there all the time. The floor sloped downwards; sometimes he lurched forward because of that.

He heard Leah breathing softly.

That grew louder.

'You're nearly back,' she said and Rollison knew that she would have been surprised had he found anything to give them hope. 'It's just the shell below deck, Mr—'

'In the emergency,' he said, 'you could make it Rolly. Like my close friends.'

She didn't answer.

'And it's battened down or boarded over,' said Rollison. He did not tell her that the floor sloped because he was almost sure of the reason; the boat was settling down on one side, moving slowly but inexorably.

He turned his eyes towards the dark boards above and he could not see a thing. This was a Stygian blackness. His nerves were nagging at him. The water kept lapping. The boat was listing and, if he were right, it would soon be right under, might even turn turtle. How deep was it here?

He reached Leah again.

'A shell,' he said, 'with wooden walls.'

'Oh, God!' she exclaimed, 'don't keep *fighting*! We haven't a chance.'

He was close and put his arms about her. The strange thing was the naturalness, a sense of oneness between them.

'All right, Leah,' he said, 'don't worry too much. I want to find out if Micky's here. We'll hold hands and walk across and turn back from the far wall. We'll cover all the floor, that way. It's slanting a bit, so hold tight.'

He expected her to say that it was a waste of time. She didn't. They stepped out slowly, fearful of kicking against something; someone. Rollison and Leah Sharp, holding hands in this pitch darkness, and—

Something cold fell on Rollison's forehead. He jumped but didn't speak. He wondered whether she noticed his movement. Another drop, icy cold, touched the tip of his ear. Then he wondered whether Leah had felt the water.

Water.

It was dripping through from the boards above as the water lapped over the side. The most dreadful part was the inevitability; and the fact that he hadn't been given a chance. There had been just that biting gas, the smashing blow on the head and darkness. Now it looked as if he would be left in darkness for the rest of his life. His *life*. Minutes—or hours?

More drops fell.

'Mr—' Leah began and caught her breath again. Then, 'Rolly.'

'Yes, my sweet.'

'Can you—talk about something? Anything—anything to make me think about what you're saying. I—I've always had a horror of drowning.'

'Listen, Leah,' he said gently, 'we all have a horror of dying some way or another. It catches everyone up. The horror, I mean. I've been sitting back and waiting for death so often I've lost count and I'm alive. But it does things to you. Death's a great leveller. Shall I tell you something? From the moment I saw you, you mattered.'

She didn't speak.

'You always will,' Rollison said, quite simply. 'The beautiful Leah. If there were light to see you by—'

'Don't,' she whispered. 'Please don't.'

'It's true.'

'I—know. But please don't.'

Rollison kicked against something which yielded. He staggered. His hand was torn from Leah's grasp. He banged his head against the wall of the hold and pain shot through it. He grew steadier but his heart thudded. Leah was forgotten, beauty was forgotten.

'What—what was that?' Leah asked huskily.

'Micky,' he said. 'I think. Stay there.' Rollison dropped to his knees and crawled towards the spot where he thought the body lay.

'Body?'

He kicked against something which wasn't so solid or so heavy. He groped, blindly, without calling out to Leah, although she would know he had found something.

He touched cloth; then a hand; then a ring on the hand. His fingers moved. He held his breath for fear of what he would discover; and when he discovered it beyond all doubt, he kept utterly still, feeling as if death had already caught up with him.

This was Old Glory.

He felt for her pulse and a great exultation filled him.

She was alive.

He had brought her to this; if she lived to be a thousand he could never escape the responsibility. He'd brought here here, so he must get her away. Damn reason, damn logic.

Out of the blackness came thought of the little bag she kept in her skirt. Unexpectedly, his heart began to thud with hope. He felt for the thick folds of the skirt, touched the lorgnette then found the pocket. He slid his hand in.

She had cigarettes, she had matches, she had a pair of scissors.

'Rolly,' gasped Leah, 'don't keep so quiet, don't—'

He stood up; and suddenly his arms were about her, their bodies and their lips met in long and fierce embrace. She needed him; his assurance, his hope, his confidence. She could face death with him but not on her own.

He drew back.

They did not need to speak.

Rollison struck a match and light blazed against his eyes, the reddish yellow light from non-safety matches. He could see. He held the match upwards and it burned like an oil torch, because of the darkness it destroyed. Rollison caught a glimpse of Leah; then Lady Gloria lying on her side; and of the bare walls. These were made of stout timbers, fastened with big nails; solid timbers, a foot wide, probably three or four inches thick.

Micky wasn't here.

Then Rollison heard drops of water falling from the ceiling and looked up. But before he could see where the water was coming from, the light burned his fingers.

He dropped the match.

He could still see Leah's face in his mind's eye with her beauty aflame with fear. He could *think* of beauty.

The water kept dripping now, little sounds; plop-plop-plop-plop. He fumbled for another match. The box was half-full. He took it in his fingers, and said:

'Narrow your eyes. We want to look round, this time.'

'All right,' she said.

He struck the match and the light seemed less bright; it didn't hurt. He saw everything that he had seen before; and something else. The houseboat was listing more; water was gathering along the far side. But that wasn't all.

In a corner was an iron bar.

Rollison went nearer and found that it was an old crowbar. Water was trickling about it. Water was coming through the boards above the crow-bar more freely than anywhere else. Rollison's shoes splashed through it.

'Leah,' he said, 'look after Old Glory. I'll strike another match.' When he did so, Leah was bending down over the older woman. Rollison picked up the crowbar. The iron was very cold.

As he moved, he splashed noisily. The water was coming in much faster, would soon start swirling about their feet.

'Leah, come here.'

She came at once, wading.

'Hold the matches, will you?' he asked, for above everything else she needed something to do.

She said, 'Yes.' She joined him again and he put the matches into her hand.

'Be very careful. If you drop them—'

'I won't. But what do you think you can do?'

'I know what I can try to do,' said Rollison grimly. He waited until a match flared, then scanned the walls and found a crack between two heavy wooden planks. 'I'm going to work to widen that,' he said.

Leah didn't answer; somehow, she stopped herself from saying the obvious, the terrifying thing—if he made a hole, the water would come through faster.

But she could not fail to know the danger of that.

He thrust the point of the crowbar into the crack in the wood and began to lever the bar; to and fro, to and fro.

The iron made a groaning sound on the wood; as if their hearts were groaning.

The water fell from the ceiling; plop-plop-plop-plop.

Now and again, the scrape of a match made a new sound; and showed the glistening water on the floor, swirling sluggishly about Lady Gloria. On the listing side, at her feet, it was a foot deep.

The hole was getting larger.

Wood splintered.

Rollison worked on savagely. His hands felt almost raw. He sweated all over and his clothes clung to his back and legs. He was breathing harshly, painfully. He couldn't be sure that he was making much progress but one of the planks of wood was freer. If he could prise it out a little more, and exert more strength, he might get it right out of position, squeeze behind it and *push*. He himself could squeeze through a gap the width of one timber; but two would have to be moved to get Lady Gloria through.

The water was almost up to his ankles now.

Then the plank of wood groaned and Rollison nearly lost his balance as it moved more freely. He banged into Leah. She gasped and something dropped with a splash.

Rollison said sharply, 'What was—that?'

'The matches,' she cried. 'Oh, God, I've dropped the matches!'
In a moment of silence and darkness there was just the sinister,
dripping sound. Then Rollison moved, slid his arm round Leah's
waist and squeezed.

'I pushed them out of your hand,' he said. 'The water isn't coming
in this side. We've still time. Just keep your fingers crossed.'

Leah didn't speak but her breathing was quick, panting.

He groped, found the top of the plank where he had levered it free,
pulled against it with all his weight and forced it down so far that he
could squeeze through.

Crowbar in hand, he stepped to the gangway running round the
ship. He was free, in a few minutes all of them would be out of here.

Then he heard footsteps and voices, not far off.

CHAPTER TWENTY-THREE

Turn Turtle

ROLLISON STOOD QUITE still.

The voices seemed a long way off but the footsteps very near. He peered upwards. He could see a patch of sky touched with stars, not far away, and moved towards it.

The footsteps drew nearer.

A man said, quite clearly, 'It's listing badly but isn't right down yet. It's taking a hell of a time.'

'It'll soon be under.'

'Better cast her off.'

'Think we ought to?' a man asked. 'If it drifts over the weir, it'll be noticed, they'll have to salvage it.'

'It won't drift over the weir, only to the pool,' the second man said. 'It's deeper water there. And private property, too. Ours!' He gave a high-pitched laugh which sounded strained. 'Cast her off, can't you?'

The other man didn't answer.

There were little sounds; the lapping water, movements of feet on the ground. Rollison moved slowly towards the patch of sky, reached it and found that he was at the foot of a companionway; just a wooden ladder which rose at an angle towards the upper deck. He could climb up this and on to the deck but could he do it without warning the men? He pushed the crowbar between his leg and his trousers, then placed his hands at the sides of the ladder and a foot on the first rung.

Soon, his head was above the boards.

He turned his head and saw the men crouching by the aft of the boat. One was moving, working at a mooring rope. The other was smoking a cigarette. He straightened up.

'Hell of a time you're taking!'

'Look, if you think you can do better—'

Rollison climbed up, the slight sounds he made being drowned by their voices. He stood upright. He was within a yard of the little jetty and the men had their backs to him. He held the side of the jetty, to steady himself, and climbed on to it. A board creaked.

'Nearly through,' one of the men said.

'Oke.'

Rollison drew out the crowbar, moved forward—and trod on a piece of rotten wood. He stumbled. As he went down he knew that the others were bound to hear. He steadied desperately, if he lost this chance he would never get another.

And then he leapt, the crowbar swinging. The nearer man jumped at him at the same time. Rollison felt the jar as the iron smashed on to the man's head and heard the crunching of the skull.

The man crumpled up and Rollison turned savagely on the other, in light which came only from the stars. He could see nothing except the glitter of a raised knife and wielded the crowbar again. Steel struck it, sparks flew. Rollison raised his right foot and thrust it out. The man fell against it. Rollison pushed, the man fell back, reached the edge of the jetty, staggered—and went over.

Water splashed over Rollison, on to the boat, on to the jetty. There was a sound that might have been a scream; and then a gradual settling down, just quiet noises as if the man had lost consciousness and could not even try to save himself.

But Leah and Old Glory—

Rollison caught his breath.

One man was in the water, the other was a crumpled heap behind him. There was a widening gap between the boat and the jetty. The boat was listing away from the side; the thwarts were already above jetty level. Water was coming over on the other side more swiftly. A sudden surge and it would turn turtle, carrying Old Glory and Leah out of life.

Dare he jump on board? Could he, without giving the boat the motion needed to make it sink?

He *had* to.

He drew back, poised to run and to jump, then took a flying leap. He landed, staggered and pitched forward. He banged his head but it didn't knock him out. He stood up, unsteadily, fearfully, and made his way to the gap he had torn in the side.

He heard movement.

Leah was trying to drag Old Glory through.

'All right,' Rollison said, 'I'll take over.'

*

Rollison stood on the deck with Old Glory on the boards by his feet, Leah by his side. In the starlight they could see the bank, ten or fifteen yards away.

'You climb over and swim to the bank,' Rollison said to Leah. 'I'll take Old Glory.'

'*We'll* take Old Glory,' Leah said.

There were moments of dread; cold, clammy fear. They hauled themselves up to the gunwale, dragging Old Glory. Leah climbed over, she hauled, he pushed the older woman. Then he lowered her into the water.

Ten minutes later, cold and dripping wet, they hauled Old Glory up on to the bank.

Five minutes after that, Leah bent over the body of the man whose skull Rollison had smashed.

'It's Jake,' she said, quite steadily. 'My brother Jake.'

'He didn't work alone,' said Rollison, 'and Red wasn't with us, was he?' They were just words. Jake—Red—Sal—Jonah—Ivan. None of these mattered. He was alive, with Leah, with Old Glory. That mattered.

He heard a sound in the distance and looked up. It was a car engine followed by a car horn blowing on a high-pitched, urgent note. Some way off, headlights blazed. He saw two cars, heading this way. They drew nearer, rising up and down crazily, and he knew that they were being driven over fields, not smooth roads.

It was like a dream.

In the first car was Grice, two Yard men, and a police-surgeon; and Micky the Red Ogilvie.

In the second were local police and Jolly.

'I was in the kitchen, just ready to come out when Jake arrived,' Micky said excitedly. 'Leah, I hate telling you, but Jake—'

'I know about Jake,' said Leah.

'You'd better know, too,' said Rollison to Grice and, as he talked still almost in a dream, he watched Micky. A doctor was bending over Old Glory; it was all over.

But who worked with Jake?

'For the love of Mike go home and get some sleep,' growled Grice.

'What more do you want? You've killed a couple of men who'd have been hanged, anyhow. You've found your aunt. Your cousin and her boyfriend are obviously in the clear. We've found the dope. We know it was smuggled into the country a year ago and that Jake Sharp used some of the fairground men to distribute it. He probably did blackmailing, too. Look here,' went on Grice, 'I've got it all down in black and white.' He thrust typewritten statements at Rollison who sat at Grice's desk in Scotland Yard and smoked. 'It's all *over*. You can call yourself lucky, you ought to be drowned.'

'That's right,' said Rollison.

'And still you aren't satisfied,' Grice growled. 'How much more do you want?'

'I want to know who Jake Sharp worked with,' said Rollison. 'It might have been this chap I knocked in the river but there might be another key man we don't yet know. Certainly there was a contact man outside the fair. Micky Ogilvie might be all right and he might not. Listen, Bill—'

'I seem to have been listening to you for hours,' complained Grice, 'and I've too much to do as it is.'

'Be more selective,' urged Rollison. 'Do the right things. Lady Gloria is still unconscious and likely to be for a few hours. Someone kidnapped her, remember. I'd like to know who. I'd like to send her back to the Marigold Club while she's still unconscious. Then I'd like to see what happens.'

Grice said slowly, 'Rolly, what *is* this? If your aunt can tell us any more, she will as soon as she comes round.'

Rollison said grimly, 'You once warned me about something. Remember?'

'What?'

'Blood's thicker than water.' Rollison's voice was brittle. 'The Rollisons are a clanny lot. Old Glory might believe that she should do the Christian thing and forgive. She might believe that she can reform a strayed family sheep. I wouldn't like to be sure.'

'You mean—Sal Hardy?'

'I mean Sal.'

'But why, man?'

'If she killed her maid, she'd be scared, wouldn't she? And put the poor little frightened-lovely act on. I've been pondering on Sal since my aunt disappeared. Sal could have persuaded Old Glory where no one else could—blood being thicker than water,' he repeated grimly. 'If Sal's up to no good and the maid discovered it...'

'The cord came from Sharp's, remember?'

'I do. Sal's been to the fair a lot. Bill, call me crazy but take it from me the chief reason I've doubted if it were Sal is that she came to ask my help. If she's guilty, why take that chance?'

Grice rubbed his chin.

'We'll find out,' he said. He grimaced. 'Rolly, I've been sure it wasn't your cousin. I'd assumed she might be sheltering someone, but—'

'Who lured Old Glory away?' demanded Rollison and added, 'Let's find out before my aunt has to tell us.'

'Oh, all right,' Grice growled.

'Have plenty of men handy,' advised Rollison. 'If I'm right, Sal will have killers for friends.'

It was evening, and nearly dark.

Leah Sharp, dressed in an off-red dress which wasn't quite the right colour for her, looked magnificent as she studied the trophy wall at Rollison's flat. Rollison was sleek and only slightly bruised. When the front-door bell rang, Jolly was heard to move towards it; and soon Sal came hurrying in, bright and beautiful. She was surprised to see Leah but not taken aback.

'But how lovely to see you!' she exclaimed and gave Leah both hands to grip. 'And how happy you must be now that it's all over! And *you*, Rolly.' She took his hands and her eyes glowed. 'You may kiss me.'

Rollison kissed her, lightly.

'Pooh,' said Sal, 'you're losing your touch. You need more exercise!' Her eyes danced as she looked at Leah. Then she became serious, her eyes rounded as if in concern. 'How *is* Old Glory? The poor darling, she *must* have had an awful time.'

'Very bad,' agreed Rollison.

He did not like what he saw and heard. This wasn't a girl who was almost hysterical, certainly very excitable; she was too gay, too calm, too "natural."

'But not seriously hurt,' he went on. 'The police have sent her to
the Club, she doesn't need nursing, just needs someone to keep an eye
on her. Hilda Morant will do that.'

'Oh, I'm so glad,' said Sal. She allowed her eyes to spill over with
merriment again. 'Rolly, darling, confess how wrong you were. You
thought Micky was a villain, didn't you?'

'If I could have pounds for the wrong guesses I make I'd be as rich
as you,' said Rollison.

Sal laughed.

Sal left...

The police followed her; and Rollison, leaving Leah at the flat,
went to the Marigold Club. It was quite dark. He did not know that
Sal went to a telephone, soon after leaving his flat.

He looked down at Lady Gloria, who was sleeping much more
naturally and did not seem too ill, then went to the big old-fashioned
wardrobe in her bedroom. There was plenty of room and it had
ventilation holes. He did not close the door until he heard two sharp
rings at the telephone—an agreed signal from Tipple who was in
charge of the police inside the house.

Rollison backed inside and closed the door. The smell of moth
balls and lavender, merging together, was almost overpowering.

He watched.

He heard footsteps and then saw the door open.

He heard the door close, the key turn in the lock. Then light
footsteps came.

Yes, Sal had come.

Sal had a length of something in her right hand; a slender cord.
Was it of silk?

She went to the side of Lady Gloria's bed while making a noose in
the end of the cord. It was all so matter-of-fact. Lady Gloria's face
was turned away from her and from Rollison but Rollison saw Sal lift
the grey head and slip the cord beneath it and then round her neck.

So there it was.

Rollison pushed the wardrobe door open.

'No, Sal,' he said. 'Not this time.'

She spun round. The eyes which could be so beautiful blazed at
him with shocked hatred. She snatched at a gun in her handbag but

he reached her before she could get it out and held her fast when the police, stationed outside, broke down the door and came rushing in.

She began to scream.

She was screaming when the police carried her out of Lady Gloria's room into one nearby.

'Nice woman,' said Detective Sergeant Tipple, rubbing the cleft in his chin. 'She telephoned someone at the fair before she came here, Mr Rollison, probably sent for someone to get her out of here if she ran into trouble. Going to wait?'

'Of course I'm going to wait,' said Rollison. 'Outside the room this time.' He went into the passage.

He felt tired and shaken but excited.

Soon a word was sent up by the police watching the street. Rollison went on to the landing. He heard a maid open the front door of the big house and say:

'Good afternoon.'

'I want to see Lady Gloria Hurst, please,' a man said. He made it sound like: 'I vant to see Lady Glor-ee-a Hurst, pliz.'

CHAPTER TWENTY-FOUR

Giant's Rage

ROLLISON SAW TIPPLE'S startled and incredulous look. He had warned the police to have plenty of men at hand but no one had suggested that Ivan would come.

'You didn't guess—' Tipple whispered.

'I'm not surprised,' hissed Rollison. One thing had pointed to Sal and Ivan but this wasn't the moment to talk.

Downstairs, Ivan rasped, 'Please, I am in a hurry, it is important.'

'If—if you will wait one minute, please,' a startled maid said.

She backed away. Rollison peered over the banisters and saw her scurrying away from the giant. In the hall, he looked more gigantic than ever. He wore a tweed coat which was too large for him and the distorted view which Rollison had of his face showed pallor and tension. The tawny eyes flickered upwards but Ivan looked at the head of the stairs.

He took a step forward, as if he wouldn't wait any longer.

Then Sal screamed.

Rollison never knew how she broke loose. When she screamed, he was looking down at Ivan. It was like looking into the face of a maddened giant. Lips, eyes, nose, everything in the huge man's face stiffened and went taut; then Ivan bounded towards the stairs, uttering a roar which was frightening in itself.

A man upstairs shouted, '*Hold her!*'

'Ivan!' screamed Sal. '*Ivan!*'

A Yard man, hiding in a downstairs room, ran forward. Ivan simply swung an arm and floored him; he didn't get up. Ivan leapt to the stairs and the very house shook. He raced up.

Tipple ran towards the head of them for a head-on clash.

'Come back!' cried Rollison.

'To hell with him!' roared Tipple.

'*Ivan!*' screamed Sal. 'They're hurting me!'

Ivan reached the landing as Tipple dived for his legs. It was a brave effort but it ended as inevitably as all such efforts must. Ivan saw the Yard man coming and bent down. He picked Tipple up like a man plucking a stone from the ground. Another man was running from the room where Sal was held. Ivan flung Tipple at him bodily. The men crashed; Tipple lay still, the other rolled away, staring fearfully at the giant.

'Ivan!' called Sal in a piercing voice, 'save me, save me!'

Rollison turned, gun in hand. Two men were advancing cautiously along the passage—Ivan could crush them. The only thing to stop the giant was Rollison's gun but, if he missed, the Yard men would be hurt.

'*Ivan!*' Sal screamed and a door opened.

But she didn't appear. Lady Gloria appeared from the other room. She clutched the side of the door, her eyes looked bleary, she was very pale. She stood alone between Ivan and Sal Hardy. Nothing would keep Ivan away—nothing would stop him smashing Old Glory to pieces if she tried to stop him. But she drew herself up to her full height and said:

'I will not—'

'Glory, run!' cried Rollison desperately.

She heard him and looked startled but didn't obey. Ivan did not even look round. One of the men leapt at him; Ivan shot out a foot and sent him backwards, groaning.

Ivan was a yard from Lady Gloria, huge hands raised.

'*Ivan, help me,*' sobbed Sal.

Then Rollison leapt.

But for Old Glory, he would never have attempted it. But she was there, as helpless as a child standing in front of an express train. So Rollison leapt and clutched at Ivan's legs. It was like tugging at iron girders. Ivan kicked one leg free and raised it as if to stamp on Rollison's head.

Rollison rolled away and jumped up.

The remaining detective on the landing took a desperate chance and flung himself forward. As Ivan staggered, he struck savagely with a truncheon. Ivan shook his head, shot out a great arm but missed. Rollison went for him again. He felt himself gripped in one great arm. If Ivan hugged him, his ribs would crack. But Tipple had found his feet and lunged forward, other policemen clung on to Ivan the Terrible like limpets, gradually easing the pressure from the Toff, gradually pulling the giant down to the floor.

And all the while, Sal screamed as if madness possessed her.

*

It was another, quieter day.

Grice was in Rollison's flat, sitting with his back to the trophy wall and oblivious of it. Jolly was in the kitchen; the door was not closed. Not far away, in the Marigold Club, Lady Gloria was queening it over the residents as if her niece were not awaiting trial, after the first court hearing, on a charge of murder.

Ivan was also awaiting trial.

Somewhere in the north of Scotland, Micky the Red Ogilvie was trying to drown his sorrows. He had loved Sal but Rollison and Old Glory had persuaded him not to stay down south. All he had done had been for love of Sal and no one wanted vengeance against him.

Leah was at the fair.

It had been on the move again; was near a north-western suburb. It was a fair without its boss, without its fighting giant, without its little man with the huge hands in charge of the coconut stall, because Ed Garney and one other Sharp brother were also awaiting trial; they had all worked with Ivan from the beginning.

'It started with small stuff, months ago,' Grice said.

'Your cousin was smoking loaded cigarettes then but she never overdid it. She found excitement in distributing the stuff and watching others being wrecked by it. Her form of sadism. Then she met Ivan Waleski and they fascinated each other. Meanwhile Jake Sharp and Waleski had a runner who brought the drug in from the Middle East. Everything was going fine for her and the rest when Micky Ogilvie came along and fell in love with her. She used him to make her Ivan jealous—'

Rollison said heavily, 'Was she all bad? He could have smashed Micky to little pieces.'

'Rolly,' said Grice quietly, 'I think she's all bad. She certainly killed the maid who had discovered what she was doing. Before then, she was in trouble because of Ogilvie. He'd discovered she smoked snow at times and suspected that someone at the fair was selling it to her. To try to scare him off, he was threatened with blackmail—for a misdemeanour several years old. Instead of going and paying up, he fought back hard. He hired two or three ruffians and was prepared to take on the whole fair.

'But more trouble was brewing for Miss Hardy.

'Her uncle found out that she smoked loaded cigarettes, too—the maid told him. He came to you and Sal discovered that without his knowing. She did the only wise thing then, Rolly—*she* came to you, pretending it was because of fears for Ogilvie. That could have stood up to inquiry.'

'She's clever, our Sal,' murmured Rollison, sadly.

'By then there was a lot of alarm at the fair,' Grice went on. 'Jonah was probing, so were you, we were around and Ogilvie was making a nuisance of himself. Miss Hardy tried two things. First she spread the blackmail talk. Ed Garney had done a little on the side for years and Ivan Waleski knew that. Second, she looked for a scapegoat. Leah was the obvious choice.

'It was easy, in a way, because Leah trusted Waleski who was quite ready to betray her. There's a story within a story there. Once he worshipped her but wanted much more than she was prepared to give. From adoration his mood turned to hatred. He was always much more clever than anyone thought. He sent the lipstick and he also put the cocaine in the flour tin.

'But the murder of the maid drove Sal to panic actions. The maid had discovered her association both with Waleski and drugs. Sal killed her—using some fairground cord because she had some with her; she'd taken a fancy to it. Then she put on her great act of being terrified. She believed that Ogilvie knew the truth; and Waleski went to his flat to kill him with more silken cord.

'At the fairground, Jake kept his end up, spreading confusion, glad to help frame Leah because she was favoured by her father when he, Jake, thought he should be second-in-command. But Sal couldn't keep it up. She couldn't stay at Lady Hurst's, either—I think her aunt terrified her. So she escaped. She'd nowhere to go, so sneaked into the fairground from the river and doped herself. If she were found by the police, she would seem to be a victim, no one would think a guilty person would be there. Ivan Waleski meant to keep her in his caravan until the fair shut down for the night. You took her away.

'The next thing is almost a family tradition,' Grice went on, gruffly. 'Old and young have the same follies. Your aunt, Lady Gloria, hoped to find out the truth. There's no doubt that her questions frightened Sal Hardy away from the Club. We know what happened. Sal telephoned Waleski and said she would get out but he must wait for her nearby, with a car. Lady Gloria followed her, imbued with this family illusion of being able to do the police job better than the police.'

Grice paused; Rollison looked politely interested.

'If Lady Gloria had called our men there'd have been no trouble,' Grice went on. 'Instead she caught up with her niece near the car. The street was empty. Miss Hardy and Waleski thought she'd overheard the 'phone conversation. So they attacked Lady Gloria and carried her off.

'That explains the final, otherwise inexplicable attempt to strangle Lady Gloria,' Grice said, 'and I hand it to you—you made it inevitable. It was Miss Hardy's one hope for Lady Gloria was bound to name her once she recovered consciousness. For some time Miss Hardy and Waleski had been living minute by minute, as it were— getting out of each difficulty as it came. After killing Lady Gloria they hoped to find a way to escape the consequences. As we know, they didn't expect the trap.'

Rollison said, 'I know, Bill.' He lit a cigarette, slowly, thoughtfully. 'They were either brilliant or imbecilic. Ivan did a wonderful best to make me think he was all for Leah when he came to the flat and—'

'He was scared in case Leah knew a thing or two and talked,' Grice said. 'Leah had to go. She nearly did, too. Waleski's almost a primitive in some ways, of course—a killer-type. He killed Jonah Sharp, cunningly incriminating Leah, because the old man suspected him. Ed Garney told us that.'

'So it's pretty well all cleared up,' Rollison mused.

'Oh, yes. With your passion for detail you'd like to know that Jake Sharp telephoned Ogilvie about the maid's death; he wanted Micky at the fair, so as to beat him up and keep him away once and for all. He was going to tell Ogilvie that he could give evidence that Miss Hardy had killed her maid—thinking that would frighten Ogilvie into keeping silent but Leah Sharp stopped Jake's little game that night.'

'And now it's stopped for good,' Rollison said, gruffly.

'Yes.' Grice stood up, briskly. 'One other thing. We've plenty of evidence against Miss Hardy and the others and won't need your aunt as a witness. You might tell her that.'

'I will,' said Rollison and smiled gratefully. 'You're good, Bill.
Found any more cocaine?'

'No,' Grice said. 'That's our one worry. Why don't you find it for
us?'

'What a hope,' said Rollison, amiably. They walked to the door.
'I'm going out too,' he said. 'Just to check that Leah's settled down
at the new fairground.'

Grice didn't speak.

Jolly, who appeared mysteriously, opened the door for them and
looked at Rollison almost wistfully, as if he were trying to say:

'I know that Miss Sharp is a very lovely woman, sir, but not for
you, *please* not for you.'

Rollison was quite sure that Lady Gloria thought the same thing.

He was equally sure that the beauty of Leah would haunt him for
the rest of his days. He could not make up his mind what to say, what
to think; he knew only that he wanted to see her again. He drove to
the fairground and it was early evening when he arrived. Most of the
fairground workers recognised the Rolls-Bentley; most grinned and
waved.

He had no difficulty in finding Leah's caravan which was near the
coconut shy.

A little black boy was in charge there, calling out in a husky but
carrying voice. Then Leah came from her caravan with that superb
grace and poise; and easy confidence.

'Hallo, Rolly,' she greeted.

'Hallo, Leah!' He looked at her and smiled his message. 'How are
you? You look as if—'

'I'm back in my world,' said Leah. She smiled, as if something
were hurting her and yet had to be faced. There was a long silence,
as if neither wanted to speak. Then she went on, 'Stay in yours,
Rolly, please. They *are* different.'

He wasn't really surprised as he looked at her steadily, knowing
that she meant it. Jolly—Old Glory—and now Leah with the same
refrain. Could they all be wrong?

'All right, Leah Sharp,' he said and dipped his hands into the box
of light wooden bails, found the heaviest he could and stood back.

'Sixpence, sah,' said the little black boy.

'Great Scott!' exclaimed the Toff, 'I mustn't cheat you, must I? He tossed a shilling into the outstretched palm. 'I'll have half a dozen!'

He took up his position and hurled one ball after the other. One missed. Five crashed on to the same coconut but did not shift it.

The little black boy's face was a study in distress. Leah hurried forward.

It must be stuck,' she exclaimed.

'Ed Garney couldn't play straight if he tried,' said Rollison and joined her.

He wasn't thinking about Ed or coconuts, only about Leah's figure, her grace, her beauty, her plea. If he called, she would come. She knew that and begged him not to call, knowing that the future could never be wholly theirs.

She fingered the coconut, pulling and tugging, until he was forced to say:

'Let me try.'

He tried.

After a few seconds, he began to forget Leah and all the things she might have come to mean. He found that the coconut was tightly jammed but the fibrous shell was cracked and something glistened beneath it.

He used his knife to chip more of the shell away; and the "something" was steel. Soon, he laid bare the whole of the steel which was covered by the coconut shell. By then a little crowd was watching and Leah was beginning to realise that already he could think more of this than of her, that there was always the magic of a problem in his life, no one woman would ever really possess him.

At last, he held a shining steel "egg" in his hand. He saw the join in the middle. He twisted—and the top unscrewed.

A little white powder spilled out.

'That's it,' he cried, 'that's the missing snow! Ed Garney hasn't had a chance to hide it anywhere else.' His eyes were glistening, he was absorbed, excited. 'What a present for Grice! Leah, we've found—'

But Leah wasn't by his side.

She was walking towards her caravan and into the evening sun.

Have you read *A Bundle For The Toff*?

When Richard Rollison brought his lovely new girlfriend back for a nightcap at his Gresham Terrace flat, passion was very much on the agenda. But could it be that the Toff's past was catching up with him? On the doormat outside his home, lay a new born baby—the result of some careless liasion, abandoned at his door.

Rollison knew it was not his child but the tongues were bound to wag—and soon. Could he find the baby's mother—and, even more importantly, its father—before he was discredited in the eyes of the world? And just how far were those who wished to see his name tarnished prepared to go?

'*Kill him*,' a man screeched and a second one leapt up, clutching at his ankle. He felt a sharp pain and then a crushing blow as a knuckle-duster punched on his instep. A club struck the bar close to his right hand, stinging his fingers.

He heard a whistle, high-pitched and loud, from somewhere outside and two or three of the men glanced towards the open door. The whistle shrilled again, as if in warning, and a man shouted:

'The cops!'

'Cops!'

'My God, the police—'

Then there came a great thudding and clattering outside in the street, men were shouting, others were swearing. Some of those in the room swung round towards the door; others, having gained it, were already rushing into the street.

The *police*? Or—

Suddenly Rollison saw Punchy Parks, not far away from him. In Punchy's hand was a knife. Beside him was another swarthy-skinned man, the Indian or Pakistani, who also held a knife—by the blade. Before Rollison had realised the extent of his danger the knife was flung at him, a glinting silvery streak. He darted his head to one side, heard the sickening sound of the blade burying itself in the wood of a bar only an inch from him. A second knife came and he saw yet another in the swarthy man's hand.

There was only one thing for Rollison to do; he jumped.

A Bundle for The Toff, published September 2004. For more details of this and John Creasey's other books, visit www.johncreasey.com